THE EXHIBITION OF

PERSEPHONE Q

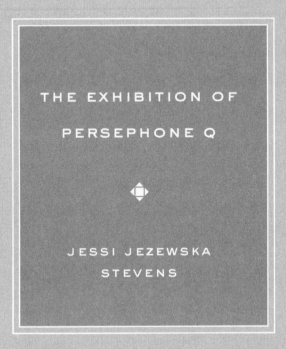

THE EXHIBITION OF

PERSEPHONE Q

JESSI JEZEWSKA
STEVENS

FARRAR, STRAUS AND GIROUX

NEW YORK

Farrar, Straus and Giroux
120 Broadway, New York 10271

Library of Congress Cataloging-in-Publication Data
Names: Stevens, Jessi Jezewska, 1990– author.
Title: The exhibition of Persephone Q : a novel / Jessi Jezewska Stevens.
Description: First edition. | New York : Farrar, Straus and Giroux, 2020.
Identifiers: LCCN 2019038069 | ISBN 9780374150921 (hardcover)
Subjects: LCSH: September 11 Terrorist Attacks, 2001—Fiction. | GSAFD:
    Psychological fiction
Classification: LCC PS3619.T4835 E94 2020 | DDC 813/.6—dc23
LC record available at https://lccn.loc.gov/2019038069

Designed by Gretchen Achilles

Our books may be purchased in bulk for promotional, educational, or business use.
Please contact your local bookseller or the Macmillan Corporate and Premium Sales
Department at 1-800-221-7945, extension 5442, or by e-mail at
MacmillanSpecialMarkets@macmillan.com.

www.fsgbooks.com
www.twitter.com/fsgbooks • www.facebook.com/fsgbooks

1 3 5 7 9 10 8 6 4 2

For my grandparents

Candid pupil, you will readily accede to my first and fundamental axiom—that a lady can do no wrong.

—MARIA EDGEWORTH,
An Essay on the Noble Science of Self-Justification, 1795

ONE

I

One night, I woke up to find I no longer recognized my husband. The room was dark and still and blue. The computer in the kitchen glowed. I had woken, as I sometimes do, in a fit of desire that was usually reciprocated, as if Misha and I were wired to the same internal alarm: we woke up as one. This was often how we began to make love. We reached for each other through the film of separate dreams and then fell back in states of mutual surprise, nonverbally reaffirmed. That night, however, he slept. The thin light spilled through the air shaft and onto our bed, and in it he looked strange. Not less attractive—if anything, more so—but also not quite like the man I'd married not so long ago. His chin was slack. His brow furrowed with some small concern. I rubbed my eyes. Misha was older than I was by only a few months, but in that moment it seemed a whole decade had intervened. I reached out to touch his cheek across a stretch of time. He didn't stir.

He always was a wonderful sleeper. On trains, in waiting rooms, sprawled across the slanted floorboards as he lay down to perform the stretches the chiropractor had prescribed for his back. Once, in July, when all the stores were filled with crowds, I left him at the deli counter to wait for meat, and when I returned, I found him dozing on a stool before the domed cases of salads and cold cuts and spreads, our order long since priced and wrapped. I tugged at a stripe on his sleeve. Then, too, he hadn't stirred, and I'd felt frustrated and alone, all on my own in the crush of the holiday crowd, freighted with grapes and milk and womanhood. I was embarrassed to find how much I cared about what the deli men would think, how to get the ice cream home. Really, I thought, is this the sort of woman you've become? I felt similarly disappointed in my humorlessness now, in bed, where Misha lay unresponsive to stimuli. I imagined what I'd say to him come morning. *You were out cold! Nothing doing!* He loved his idioms. I shifted in the sheets. I said his name, though I don't know what I would have done if he'd woken up. I had no agenda. It seemed to me that if only he moved or responded, then everything would be as it was before. I could go back to sleep. For now, I missed him acutely. I touched his face. My fingers skated across the hard, hot plane of his cheek, down the bridge of his nose. Then, in a small and violent impulse I still don't understand, I pinched his airways closed.

I am not a violent person. When I was a girl, my father often told me I ought to stick up for myself a little more. I remember he used to try to wrestle with me to impart the importance of self-defense, ignite in me some passion for survival. The only move I ever really mastered was to twist against the thumb whenever an attacker grabbed my wrist, and after this, to run. Misha, too, felt distressed by my lack of indignation. I was like damp wood that will not spark, he said, no matter the heat applied. Once, while we were walking along Central Park, after dinner, a child stole my purse. I watched him dash away down the street, his small red cap tracing a lovely, bouncing pattern along the gray stone of the boundary wall, like a paintbrush loaded with red paint. Misha threw up his arms in exasperation. What was I doing? Run! But I stood still and calmly stunned, watching the red cap fade. It didn't seem important enough.

This is all to say I was as surprised as anyone by the situation I found myself in now. I pinched Misha's nostrils. He held his breath. I waited for him to wake, protest. And then? I didn't know. It was as if the two of us had been reversed. Because, to my amazement, Misha did not struggle. He did not inhale or fight or push away. Never opened his mouth to gulp. I held on for a few seconds, a minute, two, I don't know how long. The blood mounted quietly in my ears. Still he did not stir. I don't know which of us frightened me more, Misha or myself. Then a door slammed down the hall, footsteps dissipated on the stairs. I watched my hand float away from Misha's face. I slunk out of the bed, to the edge of the room, into the corner of the kitchenette, the farthest possible point from my husband, in case that unbidden impulse tried to exercise itself again.

I hovered in the dark. I felt slightly lifted out of myself, like an acrobat suspended just above the stage. The waste bin stood solemnly in shadow. I raised the lid. The test was still there among the rest of the trash, brandishing its positive result: I was six weeks pregnant, more or less. I looked across the room at Misha. What a way to begin, I thought. I hadn't even told him yet.

I stood very still. The kitchen tiles were cool against the soles of my feet. The stove was a cold white tomb, and it shone when a taxi passed. I drew a glass of water, ran the faucet over the insides of my wrists. As I stepped away, my foot met something sharp. I looked down. There, in front of the sink, I found what had likely woken me. It was a serving bowl that had belonged to my mother, fallen from a high shelf. The large, pale shards lay scattered across the tiles. I thought of the soap operas I often heard unfolding on the TV in the apartment next door, the clatter of clichés. And that's just what Misha and I were, clichéd! Newlyweds with growing pains. I made a mental note to do something completely extraordinary as soon as he woke up. Then I crouched and ran a finger through the ceramic silt. The mess had not been there earlier, I would have noticed. I looked around the apartment for an explanation. It was withheld. Misha's desktop, the deep reds of the carpet, the cupboards, the oven, the door were all variations on the same black box. The speakers were upright, the books silent and orderly. Clean glass jars stood on the shelves in rows. The furniture seemed innocent, sanctimonious, a coven of children wrongly accused. I held my breath, listening for another presence in the quiet room, something tall and menacing, to step forward and claim responsibility. I heard nothing but the hum of the building itself, the pulse of a car radio in the street.

I pulled the chair from the credenza and stepped onto the seat, feeling along the high plank from which the bowl had fallen for some evidence of trauma to the wood. For a moment, as my hand disappeared farther into the shadows, it seemed very possible that whoever had done this would grab me by the wrist, and I would be pulled through the plaster, through the shelves, into some secret prison, like the original Persephone into her underworld. And like her, I'd probably stay. Although in my case winter would not fall to mourn my absence, the tilt of the earth would stay the same—I was not such a narcissist as that. Still, I'd always thought of that myth as having a happy ending. She hates Hades at first. Then adapts. Sometimes I think Persephone took those six pomegranate seeds deliberately. She *wanted* to stay— But I've always had a gift for extrapolation. In the real world, sometimes pottery just falls from shelves. A broken bowl was a perfectly acceptable reason to wake up in the night. That's what Misha would have said. I replaced the chair, got a broom, dutifully swept up the dust and shards, wrapping the larger pieces in a cloth in case they might be of some later use. Then I lay down on the floor and waited for morning. Unusual things happen all the time, I thought. Everyday, inexplicable things.

And yet: I relapsed. A few nights later, I went to sleep full of good intentions, only to wake up and turn to Misha. Before I could stop myself, I pinched his nose. I held his breath. We both held it, until the moment I was stunned into remission, into guilt, and became myself again. I poured a glass of water. It happened maybe four or five times in all. I didn't know what to do. I loved Misha. I even began to wonder, was it really so bad? He rose unharmed. It frightened me, however, that Misha did not struggle. I would have liked for him to struggle. I would have liked for him to shove me into the door. To yell, *What are you doing?* Instead he slept. Maybe it would have been better to confess, but it was impossible to bring up my momentary murders now. They were too much a part of me. I was afraid to go to sleep. I no longer went to bed. Our schedules drifted gradually apart, like continents into different time zones, until there was hardly any overlap at all. I went to sleep when he woke up. I lived nocturnally and slept alone. Still my husband did not respond.

I am fully aware that Misha's and my decision to marry will strike—did strike—the people close to us as rash. We'd tied the knot only recently, in late October, when Lower Manhattan opened its gates to the general public again. I checked my horoscope; the day was auspicious for love. Other people must have felt the same. At City Hall, the queue spilled through the doors and onto the municipal steps, and I felt at one with the crowd, which I imagined to have gathered like us on the whim of proposals not yet twenty-four hours old. Traffic cones were placed every which way, trees released poisoned leaves to the green, a light northward breeze perfumed the air with drywall dust and soot. The proceedings were efficient, almost abrupt. The witness clapped when Misha and I exchanged our tarnished rings—rings that Misha himself had found buried in the Rockaway sands—and it was only then, as we were emerging from the courthouse, hand in hand, that I felt the first stirrings of surprise. I looked around. There ought to be some other queue to join, I thought, for the only just married. But there were no more forms to fill, no more lines in which to stand. We were free to go. I took Misha's arm.

(The nebula, only recently conceived, would also have been present then.)

At the time, I'd known Misha all of four months, long enough to understand that he was not, as they say, "all there." Then again, neither was I. I was suspicious of anyone who still claimed a stake in normal. Who was to say what constituted "all there" when we looked south and saw the great gap tooth against the gullet of the sky? I admired the way Misha sank beneath the surface of a day to reach a deeper kind of calm. He carried a metal detector as casually as a cane, rode the A train to the end of the line to sift through the tiny treasures that the Rockaways, like some obliging oyster, betrayed. He eschewed mail order and raffles and instant messaging (they'll steal your data, he said) and spent his afternoons bowed over the altar of the keyboard, tapping out lines of code. He lay motionless on the floor for hours, thinking up new problems to solve. As is the habit of a mathematics Ph.D. I respected it. Though it raised for me questions of an epistemological nature: Did the problems already exist before Misha articulated them, or did he instead conjure them into being, ipso facto making the world more problematic than before? Be careful of your karmic balance, I warned. My psychic says— Misha cut me off. I know what your psychic says. I will point out to her that I am solving *your* problems all the time. This was true, I was often a problem to solve. For thirty-three years I had been bringing problems into the world simply by breathing and responding sentiently. Misha calmed me down.

That is, he used to, until the night his slumber drew from me an aggression that, to this day, I do not recognize as my own. At night, I slipped out of bed, across the floor, took my keys from the hook. I didn't trust myself to be in the room.

So began my life as a somnambulist. Through November, whenever Misha went to bed, I ventured around the block. I did the shopping, went on endless walks. I sat in the diner down the street, drinking flavored coffee, hazelnut and Irish cream and other variations it wouldn't have occurred to me to try until after midnight, when—why not? During a detour to the laundromat, I studied the infomercials on the TVs mounted over the dryers. I was lulled by the sound of the machines soaping up the clothes, the manufactured scent of mountain springs, the manicured hands that maneuvered the red buttons of a blender on all three screens at once: a trio of zucchinis went to shreds. *1-800-BLENDIT!* I traversed the edges of the park, whose lawns dulled to a shadow at my left, a dark so thick it felt like something I could disappear into forever—I suppose that's why they close the parks after 1:00 a.m. People often assumed I was lost. They mistook me for a student. I stalled outside a bodega, trying to remember what it was I'd gone out to buy. Keep your head up, someone called. I watched him disappear down the dappled neon street. Thanks, I replied.

I was the sort of person who accepted rather than shaped her circumstances. My life was a long hallway punctuated by a series of open doors. I wasn't used to obstacles—not that that's how I viewed the nebula, of course. There was no question as to whether I would keep it. And yet, there was this hesitation. One night, before I stepped out into the streets, I pushed a second test (still positive) deep into the trash, buried it with paper towels. I glanced at Misha asleep in our bed. Omission was not the same as denial, I thought, which in turn was distinct from a lie.

When I was feeling adventurous, I caught the crosstown bus to visit my friend Yvette. Percy, she said, astonished in her scrubs. What are you doing out? She was a surgeon and was always up, though hardly available. But the hospital had an excellent cafeteria, I thought. We met for tea and quiche and cake. Sometimes I strolled all the way to the pub on 149th, for jazz. One crowded night, as I shoved through the door, I pronounced, I'm pregnant! It was the first time I'd said it aloud. And what a magical effect! People made room. Once I found myself at a table with an elderly gentleman whose knees were bad, he couldn't dance, though he used to, professionally. I asked him if he missed it. His face opened, like a fresh egg cracked onto a plate. He told me that back in the day, after rehearsal, you grabbed whatever it was you had: hot shorts, ball gowns, heels. There was red night, blue night, voguing night. The themes were decided the evening of, and news spread by word of mouth. You could be anyone you wanted back then, he said. But those clubs had all closed down. Someone offered me a seltzer. And what do you do? he asked. I reached into the pocket of my pink trench for a cigarette, then withdrew my hand. I felt I could instantly fall asleep, fade out like the shiver of the cymbals. I pinched my palms, sipped through a straw. I'm married, I told him. I'm a mom.

When the rain chattered rudely on the sill, I stayed in. I stood in the center of the room, resisting the urge to join Misha in bed, afraid my hands, of their own free will, might very well try to suffocate him again. I placed them on my hips and looked away. My gaze alighted on the shelves. One night, it occurred to me to rearrange the items on them. They rose floor-to-ceiling and were filled mostly with Misha's things. Glass jars glinted with treasures he had retrieved from the Rockaways, door hinges, pennies, rings encrusted with sand. A chessman army held its ranks. I remembered Misha's confusion when he first confronted all the empty space that used to occupy these shelves. Percy, he'd said. Where are all your things?

I did have a few keepsakes, actually. They were stored in a soapbox near the floor. I knelt and brought them out. A set of Russian nesting dolls, a copper Buddha statuette, the remains of my mother's serving bowl, wrapped in a cloth. Also a marble brick, cracked in half. It was the remnant of a church that had been struck by lightning years before. There had been a terrific storm. I'd shut the windows and gone to bed, and in the morning the sky was a terrible blue, the sun was bright, and everyone was outside, standing on the corner. The church, sandstone, was dusty rose, and a tall iron fence ran around the lawn, which on that day was dotted delicately with debris. Through the ruching of the roof, torn open as if by a serrated knife, you could see straight through the halved bricks to the bell. The rumor was a man had died, he'd been caught beneath the rubble when lightning lanced the steeple. And what could he possibly have been doing, out in a hurricane? He wasn't even homeless. We stared at the deep soot stain. Slowly, the crowd began to thin. People had to buy milk, go to work, take their children to school. I took a long walk around the block. When I returned, the spectators had cleared, and in their place I found the anemic marble brick with its bluish, marshy veins. It seemed imbued with inarticulable wisdom, a silent bodhisattva. I took it home. Now I placed it beside the Buddha himself and stood back to admire my arrangement. The artifice struck me as profound. I glanced at my husband, fast asleep in our bed. Then I reached for my keys and stepped into the rain.

Where were you last night?

Misha was at the sink, combing his hair. Damp locks conspired into rivulets.

Oh, out, I said.

His eyes met mine in the mirror.

I was gathering impressions. For future use. Like Proust.

Misha frowned.

Maybe you should try to sleep.

He kissed my cheek. As soon as he comes home, I thought, I will break the news. I went about my chores, my own work, buoyed with conviction. When I looked up again, however, it was night, and Misha was asleep.

It troubled me that I was a threat to my husband. Violent impulses slumbered in my limbs. I brought this dilemma to the attention of my psychic in the small hours before dawn. She emerged as a shimmer from the dim of her office, draped in a satiny dress. Percy, you hidden gem. Take a seat, she said. I complied. I had not always been the sort of person who consults the stars, the positions of the planets, who links her menstrual cycles to phases of the moon, but recently I found myself receptive to any ideology that might tame my life. Perched plushly on a pouf, I traced idle patterns on the upholstery and explained how I couldn't eat, couldn't sleep, how exhausted I was all the time. That there was this impulse in me to flee— My psychic sent me a long look, as if I were withholding information. I stared at my palms, where life lines splintered. I was obedient by nature, she herself had told me as much. What reason had I to lie? My psychic kneaded her lips, deepening the red. Okay, she said. Then she lowered the lights and took the pouf across from mine. I sat very still, surrounded by clichés, globes and Ouijas and tarot cards, the red velvet curtains on the walls. She thought I had a spirit in me, and the idea was to coax it out. I nodded. I watched as she extended both hands and reached for the air between us, like a weaver for her loom. I felt something dislodge in me and slide an inch her way. It pressed right up against my throat and made it hard to swallow. Then it stopped. My psychic opened her eyes, shook her head. It's blocked. You'll have to come back, she said.

Later, as I was traipsing through the abandoned playground across the street, I realized she might have been detecting the nebula all along. I paused and closed my eyes. It seemed to me a life ought to register all at once, like an anchor sinking into sand. In practice, however, it's more like swallowing a single grape and trying to detect a shift in appetite. There isn't any change.

After a night wandering the streets, I often came home to look things up online. Misha had installed the computer in the kitchenette in late September, carrying it up the stairs like a wounded pet and plugging it into the wall. That's it, he said. And so a quiet revolution began. I had a sort of love affair with Microsoft Encarta.

I looked up facts, learned the lingua franca. *Lol.* Boolean logic was a bit of a thrill, sorting the world via OR AND NOT—I was a natural surfer of the internet. Once, with a previous lover, I'd visited a deserted island off the coast of Nova Scotia. The day was endless and grim, and as the boat pulled away into the dark waters of the Atlantic, I looked back and was overwhelmed, really, by the idea that I would never see this place again. I looked up that island now. There it was, only slightly less worth the journey than I recalled. I searched for Misha and found his results were mostly in Cyrillic. His picture loaded slowly on the screen. A younger version of himself, standing tall on a rock, addressed the camera with disdain. By way of an internet translator: *Local Chess Champion Wins Graduate Scholarship in United States.* I was very proud of Misha's brain.

I myself made little impression on the internet. I spelunked Napster. Visited beauty blogs. I still harbored hopes of becoming beautiful one day, and because such fantasies are more difficult to restrain online, at night, I indulged in searches for cosmetics. I researched waxing kits, DIY. The pink box glowed on the screen. I scrolled to the bottom of the page and in the comments recorded a footnote of my own: *How often do you have to, you know . . . ?* I shouldn't have had to ask. I worked for an author of self-help books on intimacy and sex, and she was prolific on any number of subtopics in her field: how to touch, how to talk, how to commit to oneself. Somewhere, I'm sure, she'd covered how to wax. I handled her fan mail, the filing, the bills. I proofed the drafts. No matter how many self-help manuscripts I edited, however, I remained immune to the genre's premises. On-screen, the pink box made a quarter turn. It quarter turned again. I would have liked to consult my employer about waxing kits, my abuse of Misha's airways in the night. Only I was too shy, and she was too close; she lived just downstairs. I navigated to her website now, where we'd engineered a message box for fans to write to her directly, anonymously. The anonymity was key.

> what does it mean if someone accidentally tries to suffocate a husband?
>
> (unsuccessfully, of course.)

I paused. The cursor blinked.

> i'm really not a violent person, i don't think.

My missive folded into itself and disappeared. I was less than hopeful about receiving a reply. The task of responding to such inquiries had lately been delegated to me.

Percy Q, I should mention, is not my real name. One night, not long after my psychic had tugged at some metaphysical handle in my throat, I came home from wandering the streets and searched for myself—my legal self—online. I was nowhere to be found. There were only the other women with whom I shared a sobriquet. The name my mother gave me is in fact unremarkable, plain to the point of cruelty, as if she wanted me to disappear. It is a name to share with many others. There was a porn star in Arizona, we looked not at all alike. (Indeed she'd been waxed thoroughly.) I found a scientist at the NIH who'd won awards for cancer research. A librarian in Alabama who'd waived a deceased woman's fees. They were doing important work, these women. Even the porn star, I thought, brought daily into this world some kind of urgent joy. And what had I achieved? I looked around. At the papers strewn about, the notes posted to the wall, reminders from Misha to me, and from me to him, to buy potatoes, bread, to do the laundry on Saturday, when we had no other plans. On-screen, by contrast, the porn star struck a powerful beachside pose, her smooth knees sparkling in the sand. I wondered if anyone had ever thought to look me up and mistaken me for one of these women. Not this buxom siren, maybe. But the librarian, the scientist? I asked Misha in the morning, when he woke up. Misha, I said. Do you think I could have been a scientist? He was brushing his teeth. He thought for a moment, spat a bit of foam. I can see this, he said. You have an investigative streak. He dried his face by bringing his mouth straight to the towel hanging from a ring mounted on the wall, then kissed my cheek. The door sighed shut. I always felt Misha's absence most acutely right after he left for Insta-Ad. I loved him, I really did. Only I didn't want to kill him. That was all.

2

I did not need to check my horoscope to know that this was not a particularly promising moment to bring a nebula into the world, not for me specifically, nor for the nation in general. We were at war. The skyline had thinned. Anthrax accented the nightly news, and frankly, it was not hard for me to imagine why or how or whether terror would strike again. Don't say that, Misha said. It was Saturday, and we were at the credenza, sharing an afternoon tomato. The sheets were at the laundry, set to tumble dry. Misha was reminding me that I lived in one of the safest countries in the world, in one of the most powerful empires known to man. I nodded. This was less comforting than it might otherwise have been, considering the assaults that Misha himself had endured, unknowingly, in bed.

In the fridge, I found two fruit-on-the-bottom yogurts: dessert. I peeled away the silver skin from one and set the other aside, plus a spoon. Misha was on the bare bed, deep in thought, arms and head draped over the edge of the mattress in a posture designed to promote blood flow to the brain. I wondered if he looked different. Dark curls brushed the hardwood. The whites of his eyes were wide. But everyone looks a little alien, I thought, when his face is upside down. I considered the armory he had brought with him when he moved in, the glass jars, the metal detecting wand, the textbooks and CDs. My feelings for Misha had not changed. They were still there, like a bowl on a shelf. An impossible shelf, too high to reach. I pushed the empty yogurt cup into the trash, paused. Then I lifted it out, added it to the milk jugs in the recycling bin.

Misha, I said. Do you feel different at all?

He thought for a moment.

I don't think so.

I nodded.

Me neither, I said.

◆

I do not know whether insanity attracts more of the same, or if it only serves to bring an extant excess into focus, but either way, in the months leading up to the attacks, it seemed to me the whole nation was under construction, page not found, the open source codes of common sense irrevocably hacked. I remember one morning, in late July, I watched a woman spill a drop of coffee on her cream-colored blouse. She looked down at the modest stain, the light changed. She pulled the silk away from her body and poured the remainder down the ruffled bib. Later, I looked into the air shaft outside our window and found a deposit of paper cranes; they gathered against the brick like bright and fallen leaves and were soon pulverized by rain. The world had become the sort of demonic place where lattes and cranes and even buildings fall, such that when they did, a part of me resisted any feeling of surprise, as if I ought to have expected it all along.

Misha and I met during this time. A few months before the towers sublimated into a too-blue sky, I responded to an ad at the library. *Thesis editor needed. New and exciting opportunity!* I was always on the lookout for lucrative, undemanding tasks. I applied. I took the train to Astor and followed Avenue B to the HQ of Insta-Ad, LLC, which at the time was also Misha's home. It was a different world in there. The attic office had once occupied the rafters of an Orthodox church, and the windows were still fitted with stained glass. Now computers lined the walls, and wires sprouted from every outlet. Ethernet cables in red and yellow nuzzled into notches meant for phones. His bed was by the window. He sat on the mattress. I sat on the chair. He apologized for the mess. But we are not getting many visitors, he said. He swept an arm toward the rows of monitors, and this was the full extent of an office tour: Behold the future of online shopping. *Insta-Ad.* I looked around. There were only two people in the entire company, Misha and his thesis advisor, and I wondered how many computers a single employee could reasonably use at once. The idea, he explained, was to close the gap between a click and the time it took a web page to load and—wham!—shellac the sidebar with a billboard meant just for you. I nodded, not understanding at all. He planned to publish and defend a dissertation on the collection and sale of consumer data. And that is where you come in, he said. I'm afraid my grammar is not so good.

I had okay grammar. This was how I made my living. I wrote odd copy for websites and galleries, anyone, really, in need of public-facing prose. The self-help author kept me on retainer. I worked out of her apartment one, two, seven days a week. Sometimes there was no work at all, and so it wasn't my fault if I seemed to be without responsibilities or income, if I had time on a weekday afternoon to voyage to the library, the Met, down the 4-5-6 line to the electric offices of Insta-Ad.

I took Misha's thesis home and brought it back marked up in red. I said, I have no idea what it means, but the grammar should be correct. He flipped through the pages I had proofed. Fantastic, he said. He thought everything I did was worthy of applause. And I liked spending time with him, marking up sentences I couldn't understand. I sensed in Misha's life an order absent from my own. He woke each day in the twin bed by the office window, stretched, spooned grounds from a Café Bustelo tin and poured the freshly brewed joe into another—there were a great many Bustelo tins around. I filled them with flowers. Absorbed at his computer, he reminded me of my psychic before her crystal ball. And mathematics itself was a language, I was learning, with a grammar all its own. Notation unraveled into incomprehensible words: product of 1 through k over product of 1 through $(n-k)$ times k to the power of n. As you can see, there is something seriously wrong with our random number generator, Misha said. He transliterated my name. There were two Discmans between us, and whenever I fell into a forlorn mood, Misha slipped CDs into both and brought me down to the street, where we pressed play as one. Just to try, he said. The music that streamed through my headphones was Hungarian Dance in G Minor, by Brahms. I smiled. It was true, as Misha said. Everything became a little comical, a little absurd, when set to the soundtrack of Hungarian Dance. I felt superior watching other people hurry through their lives. The city became a length of reel snipped from silent film, melodramatic, halting, and poorly spliced. It never occurred to me that was how I looked most of the time.

I felt less superior listening to Hungarian Dance alone, without Misha. When I returned home from my midnight rambles, I stood in the street and slipped the headphones from my ears. I looked up at our building. I thought of Misha inside, asleep. I wondered, sometimes, what others might make of our present predicament, whereby we were rarely in the same room at once. A limestone ledge jutted like a sore lip from the brick facade and ran around its girth. I followed it to Harold's former window, still surprised, after all this time, to find it dark.

I'd moved to Morningside long before I ever met Misha. Then, too, I never slept. I had a can opener and a desk and a mattress on the floor, too many thoughts in my head. I got up to walk them off in the night, like muscle soreness, or love handles. You girls are always exercising, said my neighbor across the hall. I went to the cathedral, the seminary, Grant's Tomb. There was a residential high-rise scheduled for Columbus and 107th, but development had stalled due to a spike in crime. I walked to the wasteland of the construction site, where the maze of steel beams rose into the floodlights.

I often forgot my keys on those walks. For years I hadn't needed them. I'd lived with other people, and they were always there to let me in. Things hadn't worked out, and so I was going through a bit of an adjustment with respect to entrances and exits. It wasn't long before I found myself stranded on the stoop in the nether hours between midnight and dawn. I went around back to look up at my darkened window, a little black square that meanly reflected the light of the moon. How easily identifiable my window was. And yet, like a satellite, unfathomably far. I walked a little more, to the void of the park, stamped into the city grid like a second night. Then I returned home to my new address and sat on the stoop to wait. It must have been three or four in the morning before I finally decided to try ringing my neighbor across the hall. At the time I didn't even know Harold's name. He was no more than an alphanumeric phenomenon, 4C, who'd once helped me to carry in a chair I'd nicked off the street. I looked up at his window now and saw it glowed softly with the light of a lamp. What did I have to lose? I laid a thumb into the call button. A pause. A question crackled on the intercom. Hi, I said. Then the door buzzed, the lock clicked, and I was on the stairs.

Most of what I knew about my neighbors I'd picked up by accident. The psychiatry student one door down watched soap operas on the weekends and on weekdays vomited after breakfast, again after lunch—I could hear her through the walls. The notary public who lived upstairs couldn't swallow properly, he had a click in his throat. We shared an umbrella one snowy evening while walking home from the train, and afterward I couldn't remember a single thing he'd said, I'd been so distracted by the way he seemed, quite literally, to be choking on his words. As for Harold, he had a cat, or so one assumed—the umbrella stand outside his unit was cast in a feline shape—and he struck me as the sort of person who wouldn't forget to knock on a hapless woman's door (e.g., mine) if there were ever sign of a gas leak in the night. One morning I rose to find him in a pair of red rubber gloves in the hall, holding both his recycling and mine. He pointed to the milk cartons shifting softly in the plastic sack. These go separate, he said.

He became, for a time, my only friend. I took care of his cat on weekends he went away. I babysat his niece. He was a cartoonist who lived alone, and while it's possible I appreciated his company more than he did mine, sometimes, when I went over to return his key after he'd been gone, he seemed content to let me linger. He'd pause in the door, then step aside. There's no getting rid of you, Percy, he said. I liked to poise at the drafting table by a bowl of fruit while he emptied his pockets and unshouldered his bags. On the drawing boards, he was forever investing household objects like teacups and saucers with life, illustrations bound for the pages of a children's book. I wondered why it was we encouraged, in children, the substitution of the human with the inanimate world. He ran comics, syndicated cartoons: the perspective panned from one water tower to another, another, alternately thin and squat and fat, while in the final frame a distant fellow atop a wedding cake high-rise called, *Potluck over here, one hour!* His other characters were all police. *He had his hood up*, an officer protested, still waving his gun, *I couldn't tell he was white!* I sat soberly by the fruit, officers juxtaposed against a tea service that talked. Harold polished an apple, patted my sleeve. Come on, Percy, lighten up.

Hey, I said. Can I have a can opener? You know how it can be. There are neighbors who make love so loudly you can hear them through a set of earplugs and even the floor; who walk indoors all day in heels, clacking above your head; students on Ritalin or E, and men who indulge in lecherous stares, who ask to borrow a hammer, a screwdriver, a blender, an endless list of items that are transferred from your apartment to theirs in the hope that one day you, too, will stay behind (and indeed I'd relinquished a great many useful tools to 6F this way, including my own can opener, although this was no real loss; I preferred my apartment spare, and by now I was mostly eating out of jars). I figured I was more or less par for the course, as neighbors went. Believe me, you're not, Harold said.

I had a friend once who, hearing violent sounds from the other side of her bedroom wall, a chorus of screams and curses and the hollow thump of bodies colliding with solid objects (like the wall itself), assumed a crime drama, turned up her music, and went to sleep. This terrified me. What if she was wrong? What if that woman had been me? *It wasn't you*, she said. *And what if I was right? I'd be that idiot knocking on the door at night* . . . I was grateful, in other words, to live so peaceably across the hall from Harold, especially in those years when I still lived alone. He was the sort of person who could tell the difference between television and real life, he'd let you in when you found yourself locked out. And I was always locking myself out. Night after night, I buzzed. Harold replied. We carried on a silent back-and-forth at odd hours of the dark. Even after Claire, his wife, moved in, I depended on Harold to unlock the door. Then one night he didn't answer. I buzzed. I buzzed again. I waited a long while. In frustration, I planted my hands against the glass. The bolt gave way to nothing more than the soft force of my palms. I simply drifted in.

In the morning, I lay in bed for a long while, staring at the white tin ceiling. I ought to become more self-reliant, I thought. I shouldn't depend so much on others anymore. From now on, 4C and I would lead more separate lives. Resolute, I went out for milk. From the front steps I could see the deli and the park. The dogwoods bloomed. The world seemed very manageable to me. I had my keys. Then I realized I'd forgotten my wallet. I was just about to turn back to retrieve it when I was stopped by the purple streak of a woman in a windbreaker. It was Claire, sudden as a breeze. She collided with my shoulder. I felt her fingers press into my skin. Had I seen him?

Who? I said. Her face was swollen with lack of sleep. The fabric of her jacket draped and sang. Harold hadn't come home the night before, and she was ready to call the police. I gently extracted her nails from the flesh of my arms. I'm sure he'll turn up, I said.

In Morningside, tenants were always moving in and out. Students shuffled cargo up and down the stairs, they stayed for nine months, six. Then they were gone. People, in other words, were constantly disappearing, but never quite permanently. They turned up again in delis, subways, in line at the grocery store. Harold's absence, I was sure, would be of a similarly reversible order. Of course, there were exceptions. The self-help author had passed along a cardinal rule: never let a man follow you through the door or up a set of steps, rather, make sure *you* are in a position to push *him*, in self-defense. This was all fine in theory. But from the stoop, where the storm door swung wide without regard for locks, and cathedral bells bellowed and rolled uptown, bright yellow sounds that blurred in the avenue, and where children played at recess across the street, I had trouble taking Claire's fears seriously. She was convinced: Harold had been kidnapped. I followed her inside, certain he'd be back within the night.

Harold didn't turn up that night, however. Nor the night after that. In the weeks that followed, and at my behest, those of us who could convince Claire to open the door brought her dinner. Dishes piled in her kitchen like morbid trophies as she sat by the phone, making calls to the police. I encouraged her to eat. I lifted a foil corner from a casserole, inserted a fork. Tenants lingered in the halls.

Everyone seemed to know something about the case. One woman recalled seeing a man who walked with one leg and ran with the other, at war with himself—could he have been the culprit? No, the self-help author said. That's only Buck. The notary public found it strange that Harold had forgotten to take down his trash. Meanwhile, the lock on the front door had broken the very evening of his abduction. This seemed a crucial clue. The police, however, were unconvinced. To them, Harold's disappearance wasn't a disappearance at all. These were the facts: His bank account had been emptied just days before he vanished, his assignments at the magazine wrapped up. His crayons and sketchbooks had absented themselves from his drafting table, whose proximity to the window afforded a comprehensive view of our Morningside street, a perfect vantage, the police pointed out, for departing at a moment when there were no witnesses. Finally, men of familiar size and shape and disposition had been sighted boarding planes at JFK. Statements described a certain felt jacket, olive-green, a misplaced ticket, tortoiseshell frames. Lighten up, the man had said, searching through his pockets and holding up the line. By all accounts, Harold had gone of his own free will. At night, I stood in the street, looking up at the facade. I studied the opaque windows for some sign of life. Claire was never up so late.

It was hard to say which outcome was worse for Claire, the one in which Harold endured who knows what in an outer-borough basement, or the one in which he was alive, safe, and no longer in love. Years later, when Misha moved in, she was still refusing to give up hope that Harold had been taken. She installed new bolts on the door and kept it locked. For a while we knocked in vain, then we stopped knocking at all. And I suppose that is how casually one version of reality detaches from the truth; it peels away naturally, like damp wallpaper in a neglected room.

These days, returning home from the hospital, or jazz, I often paused for a moment in the stairwell before letting myself through my own door. I wondered if something of what had happened to Harold was happening to me. Perhaps he'd woken up one night to find he didn't recognize his partner, he hardly recognized himself. He fled. Except I loved Misha, I loved Morningside. I had nowhere else to go.

◈

One night, in early December, the nebula now ten weeks along, I ran into the self-help author while I was waiting for a sandwich at the deli. I was just counting out my change when she rushed in, breathless and wrapped in multiple layers of down. I was surprised. The self-help author wasn't usually out at this hour. For a moment I thought maybe I had missed an appointment, there was an emergency, I'd forgotten to show up for work. It had happened before. A jug of laundry detergent dangled from her hand, leaking blue fluid onto the floor. She tightened the cap. Guess what, she said. I didn't guess. She told me anyway. I think I saw Harold in the laundromat.

She stood before a wire rack of Hostess Honey Buns, bouncing one package against the rest. I watched the icing smear inside the plastic. This was the first Harold sighting in some time, and I was skeptical. Was she sure? Quite sure. Felt jacket, corduroy pants. And he had a pen in his pocket, she said. One of those illustrator's markers with the tapered, felted tip. I said, You could see all that? She nodded. I swear it's him.

I followed her into the laundromat, where the infomercials were going strong. Above the dryers, the row of TV screens flickered: electric can openers conquered tins of pinto beans and tuna, one by one. I watched a woman lift a gray sock from the floor. There was always someone in the laundromat, no matter the hour, and as I took a turn through the machines I spotted a few other people sorting clothes and change. None of them was Harold. The linoleum tiles were streaked with salt and mud from winter boots, and the sharp scent of powdered soap transported me to the snowcapped mountains of a detergent box. The coin machine was decorated like a Christmas present—at the top, a bow. I peered into an alley off the main room, which held an overflow of dryers and steel tables for folding sheets. It was uninhabited. I rejoined my employer with a shrug. She shook her head. I could have sworn it was him, she said. I guess he's already gone. The overhead lights were harsh. I closed my eyes. I tried to remember Harold as I'd known him. His uneven, swaying gait. The pen. The soft echo of milk cartons gathered in the hall. The self-help author slipped another quarter into the slot, and I waited with her for a set of curtains to dry. She reached for the remote. The infomercials cut away to a press conference where the mayor was reasserting that everything was just the same as it had always been: in spite of recent anthrax scares, we refused to be afraid. I turned to the self-help author, suddenly too tired to disagree. Maybe you're right, I said. Who was I to undermine her certainty?

Outside, warm drapes pressed against our breasts, the self-help author and I turned up the avenue. We passed the playground, the church, the former chapel with its chocolate brick. As we mounted the stoop, I glanced at Harold's former window. A single lamp was on. The self-help author frowned.

By all means, she said, don't mention this to Claire.

I helped her loop clean drapes onto brass rods. Then she stood me in the doorway and sprinkled something in the air above my head: a parting charm. The scent of her laundry followed me upstairs, into the kitchenette, where, at the credenza, I separated the deli sandwich into two half-moons of silver foil. Tomato-egg-and-cheese on rye, for Misha and me to split. I set his half aside. Then I sat down at the computer to search. I typed in Harold's name. Portfolios of his cartoons appeared. Here was the essence of a man reduced to an image bank. I scrolled. It occurred to me that whether or not the self-help author had been mistaken, Harold was, in many ways, more present than I. In some ways he hadn't vanished at all. He could be summoned forth, reproduced in a few keystrokes. As for me, when I entered my own name *(NOT "porn" NOT "NIH" NOT ("cancer" OR "science"))*, the results page returned a blank. It might have even stayed this way. Then the package arrived.

4

That morning, I'd gone out to buy a set of knives. The idea to update my cookware had come to me suddenly, as I was standing in the kitchenette. The pantry doors were open, and I gazed in, unmoved by what I saw. The jars of kimchi, the sacks of grain, the pair of apples to which I'd so looked forward had all completely lost their aura. I poked at a package of dehydrated noodles. Though I was hungry, I seemed to have lost my appetite for everything I loved.

I looked down. At the open neck of my T-shirt, my veins ran blue and bright across my chest, diverting nutrients to the nebula. What do you want? I wondered at it. Then I grabbed my keys and stepped outside.

At the kitchen store, caches of cutlery hung from temporary hooks. I perused the blades. I had in mind something simple and elegant, something suited to slicing the long spine of a leek, say, or chopping walnuts into chalk. For me the path to becoming a better cook would begin with soups and stews and crudités, plenty of chopping vegetables into bits, and so I went from store to store, handling the more discreet and delicate blades. I learned the meaning of "to spatchcock" and indeed witnessed a demonstration at an upscale cooking store. (Christmas was weeks away, and people had ducks in mind.) I learned what any cutlery enthusiast will tell you, that against the skin of a tomato, a dullish knife is no better than a spoon. I met a man who vacationed by the sea and who always traveled with his own set of knives, so anathema to him were the blunted instruments one finds in an ocean turnkey. I saw stiff boning blades with titanium tips, steak knives designed to slice through even the thickest cut of meat, electric butter knives that warmed to cube the coldest stick of butter. I became distracted, for a moment, by a stack of lovely colanders that nearly toppled when I touched it. Can I help you? No, no—I was only here for knives.

The last shop I visited was small and dim and specialized. The knives shone on velvet trays and under glass, like rings. A saleswoman led me up and down the darkly glinting aisles. So, she said. What is it you like to cook? I glanced at a row of cheese guillotines strung with wire. I told her the truth. I honestly don't know. But I am about to have a baby, I said. I aimed to be prepared. She nodded. Is that right? I wondered how it was she'd done her hair, if she ate her breakfast over the sink, how it is, really, that someone finds herself in the business of selling knives. She drummed her fingers on a case of fluting blades. Come with me, she said.

There was a demonstration room in the back with a butcher's block set with large bowls of fruit and vegetables and rows and rows of cutting boards. Together, we began to chop. We sliced apples and pears and taut tomatoes, transformed handfuls of parsley into shredded chiffon. The saleswoman showed me how to rock the blade from point to handle and back again, so that the silver edge sank, without protest, into the leather of an aubergine. She chopped like someone who never needed to eat. I was drawn to her indifference. After me, she said, and I looked on as she divided the round moon of an onion into many crescents. I learned the difference between dicing and mincing. Flecks of garlic flew. I was only just getting the hang of things when she gathered all this ostensible refuse into a tall pile with the flat of her blade and swept it into the bin. I stood stunned. Then I slowly set down my knife. I peered in at the literal fruits of our labor, the apples and onions and garlic and limes. Tomato steaks and undone aubergines. An incoherent stew. I was vindicated—certainly it was stranger than anything I'd made.

Outside, the streets were slick with ice and shoppers walked with care. On the train platform, I lingered, making all kinds of promises to myself. I lit my remaining Camels one by one and tossed them to the tracks. I wouldn't be a smoker and a mother, not like mine. I wouldn't forget my keys. I would be sensible, strict, warm, I'd keep the floors extremely clean. I glanced into the white paper bag that held my knives: I'd cook. Aboveground, I paused at the vegetable stand on the corner, for onions. Their weight felt human, cradled in my arms.

Earlier that week, someone had smashed through the bottom pane of the building door, and now the vestibule was full of glass. The upper pane was also frosted with cracks, and so as not to dislodge what remained, I had taken to threading myself through the ruined lower half. I did so now, clutching knives and onions to my breast.

———

The package was there when I emerged, settled in the slush of window shards.

Over the years I have received all kinds of mail meant for former tenants: Barbaras, Vincents, Pierres, fans of interior design and environmental-protection funds, apocalyptic newsletters whose predictions I could not support (though they seemed less alarmist to me, that winter, than they had before). This package, however, arrived without any name at all. The way it was placed, on the pretty mosaic tiles and surrounded by glass, it might have been the culprit behind the shattered door. I lifted the envelope, blew away the dust. We did not often get deliveries. Who would send something to Misha or me? All our friends lived right inside, or just around the corner. They could have saved the postage. Shards fell from the folds in the paper and trickled to the floor. The flap was sealed with professional-grade glue. There was no recipient named—just an address. The apartment number was definitely ours.

5

I stood for a while in the vestibule, package in one hand, onions in the other, trying to think of anyone who might want to target me with anthrax. Except that biowarfare came in average correspondence, not in hefty envelopes—I'd seen the photographs. I wondered next if I'd ordered anything online. Or perhaps Misha had? He was as off-the-grid as a computational mathematician can be, but even still. People change. I hesitated, traced the neatly suffocated seal. Then I tucked the package under my arm and stepped inside. I had committed my fair share of marital transgressions, but I was not yet the sort of woman who snooped through her husband's mail. One can only stoop so low.

Upstairs, the apartment was empty. A rent check fluttered to the floor when I maneuvered the key into the lock. I retrieved it from the mat. The bed was made. The pantry doors were open, and I closed them again. I arranged the knives in a row. The fruit bowl, as usual, was out of fruit, and I tossed the package over its rim. Then I tore open the net of onions. They tumbled to the floor.

Bulbs retrieved, I peeled away the papery skin and fixed a rind beneath a blade. It cleaved, and the kitchenette filled with its crisp, clean smell. I turned one raw cheek to the tile top of the credenza and sliced the pearly hemisphere into concentric loops. The net emptied and the pile of rings grew. I was pulling ahead. To think that a few weeks ago I'd been suffocating my husband, and now I was chopping vegetables—for soup! It was undoubtedly a step in the right direction. By the time I ran out of bulbs to chop, the light in the kitchen had faded yet another shade toward evening, and my breasts were heavy and sore. I set down my knives. A wave of nausea passed through me like a ghost.

When I recovered, I typed *"onion soup" AND "how to make"* into Explorer. I began to despair. I read the recipe. I read it again. The will withered within me, like an old fruit. It had been quite enough to slice the onions without having to caramelize them as well. Then there was this business with the roux. And besides, I didn't have all the ingredients at hand. I pillaged the drawer where Misha kept vials of spices and herbs, but neither thyme nor sherry was to be found in there. I searched *"sherry" AND "substitution,"* but the answer, apple cider, was no help at all. I drifted, as one does, to AOL, where the home page blitzed with deals. I checked in on the waxing kit. Some patient souls had replied:

qwerty123: how often do you have to, you know . . . ?
Fantabulist: if wondering, fuck yes it hurts.
JSTORED: oh, hun. come back when ur 18!!

I sighed. I hadn't felt eighteen in weeks.

I opened Napster to see how my favorite users' libraries were coming along. I liked peering into other people's hard drives, other people's minds (stealing, Misha said). Onyx123 stocked songs by the musical wing of Neue Slowenische Kunst. I looked them up. Albums stored in others' libraries migrated into mine. I wondered what, to Misha's algorithms, my browsing history implied.

When Misha returned, the kitchenette displayed the evidence of my abandoned search. The screen was filled with Viking shipwrecks discovered along the Nova Scotian coast, the credenza was replete with onions, whole opalescent piles, and I was at the sink, sharpening my knives. He stood for a moment in the doorway, bucket and wand in hand. Is everything all right? I held up the silver yield of my errands for him to admire. I was well on my way to becoming a cook, I announced. Or at least a sharpener of knives. Misha took my wrists and gently guided them to the table. He'd left for the Rockaways at dawn, now he kissed me and I breathed him in: onions and sea and salt. I leaned into the fact of him. His coat was cool against my cheek, and when he spoke his words muffled in my hair.

Don't be mad, he said. But just now, I'm afraid I am committing us to the poetry reading again.

Often, when Misha returned from the Rockaways, I liked to sift through his winnings with him to assess the value of what he'd unearthed. Antique lighters. Spoons. Once, a tiny thimble. That evening, however, I was annoyed. I had a great deal of affection for the self-help author, but her poetry readings were a bimonthly phenomenon I took great pains to avoid.

Misha! I said. Didn't you walk quietly?

He glanced at the door and lowered his voice.

She is always in the stairs!

This was true. The self-help author really was always in the stairwell, on her way to get the mail or a gallon of milk, haul laundry to the laundromat, and this meant we often passed her on our own way out the door. She was a woman of presence, and had a way of making people flustered. She made me flustered. Still, I was annoyed that Misha, flustered or not, had accepted her invitation, especially since we'd developed specific protocols for how to politely decline.

They dragged on for hours, these readings. There really was no "popping by" for poems. This dance of invitations extended and declined was made all the more difficult by the fact that sometimes I needed to "pop by" the self-help author's on a Sunday afternoon to ask her opinion about the rearrangement of a chapter, or to clarify a passage in book two, chapter ten. I had learned my lesson, in other words, about living above one's boss: you are always on call.

Misha turned toward the door. I will tell her it is a mistake, he said. Then his eyes rested on the package. He paused. Intrigue clouded his face.

What's this?

I reached for the envelope and held it close. Of course the package wasn't Misha's. I was seized by a feeling of protectiveness, as if he might do it harm. There was a time in childhood when I lived for the mail. The nearest mall was across the border, in Quebec, and we did most of our shopping by catalog, knew the mailman by name. Perhaps it was some sense memory, then, that caused me to cling so jealously to what I felt was mine. I turned the package round. This particular envelope was too heavy for a nightgown, a Buddha, or anything else I might have ordered for myself back when the post was still supreme, and I held it delicately, in case, in my insomniac delirium, I had impulse-ordered something made of glass. Who knew what desires my subconscious might express in the well-stocked aisles of the web? I was afraid to think what Misha might find, were he to open it.

It's for the self-help author, I said. I was actually just bringing it to her now.

Misha studied me a moment, pail swinging from his hand. He brushed the hair from my face.

Babe, he said. You look a little dazed.

6

After so many years, you'd think I'd have internalized a bit of the self-help author's advice. Be honest, she said. Communicate. Say what you mean. Perhaps it would have done Misha and me some good, I thought, as I descended the stairs, package in hand, to listen to my employer on occasion. One of the very first rules she set for readers (and which I edited, for clarity and style) was to schedule time for sex. Misha and I, for our part, hadn't scheduled a single rendezvous in our lives. Arousal for us was an unpredictable if synchronized phenomenon, and lately it wasn't really a phenomenon at all. On the landing, I pressed against the wall to make room for two men carrying a small mattress up the stairs. I lingered, listening to their progress as they disappeared overhead. One floor. Two. I tried to imagine Misha assembling a crib. He was hopeless in practical matters, almost as hopeless as I. It was something I loved about him.

That particular evening, the self-help author was dyeing her hair a shade of cherry-blossom mauve. Her door was ajar, and I breezed in. Percy, is that you? Where have you been? She emerged from the kitchenette. Her head was wrapped in cellophane, then again with a kerchief. In her hand, the mechanism of her metamorphosis: a box bearing the image of a woman whose long pink locks withstood a strong headwind. The self-help author presented it to me.

How long am I supposed to leave it in?

I squinted at the instructions.

An hour.

She checked the clock.

Well, shit. Help me get this off?

The cellophane was wound like a roll of tape—it took a moment to find the end. Hurry, hurry, she said. But what harm, really, could a few extra minutes do? Her hair poured into the sink in a sheet of ruby red. I ran the faucet and massaged her scalp until the water ran clear. Her body wedged against mine, soft and comfortable. A kind of maternal impulse welled up in me. I shifted an inch away.

All my life, I had considered motherhood in only a vague, conjectural way, and in recent weeks had reached some tentative conclusions: I did not dislike children. In fact I reserved for them a great affection; I considered them my peers. For a while, in college, I'd babysat the son of an art history professor, and I often rested my hand on the crown of his head as we waited to cross the street. He liked to inspect my hair while we sipped milkshakes at the counter, an idle exercise he completed with curiosity and dignified disgust. *Percy*, he said firmly, when once he produced a leaf. *You should really wash.* He was a quiet, imperious child who enjoyed coloring and foosball. We got along just fine. With girls, it's true, I did less well.

I was hopeless around little girls. When I used to watch Harold's niece for an hour or two in the afternoons, she'd install herself in my window with a slice of toast and a spoon and proceed to push the jam endlessly from edge to edge. After a long pause she'd look up with wide and tragic eyes to ask, Is it better to take one good bite with all the jam at once, or spread it evenly so every bite has just a little bit? What a relief to send her back across the hall. And that's the thing, with a child of your own. There is no across the hall.

The self-help author, by contrast, lived a life of perfect freedom. How many women she kept cooped up inside of her, compressed, like an infinite series composed of many terms. There was the woman she'd been in Times Square in the years before the city cleared those theaters away. She'd lived out of a stolen car, run her own shop, resided for a time in an abandoned apartment alongside Tompkins Square Park according to squatter's rights, and through those broken windows tossed Molotov cocktails during the riots of '88. Now she was a successful author, a peddler of wisdom, formerly brunette and as of that evening sporting a peremptory shade of red. That December her books were selling better than we could have ever imagined. The publisher had registered an uptick following the attacks. I felt tenderly toward these new readers. I felt I understood. It is a constant struggle, to take one's mind off things. No wonder self-help sells.

I helped her gather her fresh locks into a towel, twisting the terry cloth until it held fast. She reached for the box.

It's really red, isn't it?

I conceded.

It's pretty red.

It doesn't look like the picture at all.

It's certainly from the same *genus*, I said.

I know there's some reason I pay you, Percy, but lying isn't it. Hold on, though. I have your paycheck.

She set to riffling through the papers on her desk.

I looked around the very clean room. The self-help author's apartment was the mirror image of ours. The kitchenette to the left, the bed and bath to the right. The fireplace was just the same, its mouth closed off with bricks. Her bookshelves strained with atlases and poetry collections, catalogs from museums around the world. She made a point of selecting a few to display on the coffee table, for guests: *When entertaining, one ought to have a conversation piece on hand.* That evening she'd featured an anthology of Dickinson and a map of Prague, choices entirely appropriate for the poetry reading that she'd planned in one week's time, and which, I regretted, Misha and I would not be able to attend.

The self-help author was still sifting through papers in search of my check. I was about to tell her it didn't matter, I'd come back tomorrow, the check was not why I was here, when she upturned an overflowing banker's box onto Dickinson and Prague. Receipts and coupons and pamphlets scattered. I descended to the carpet to help gather the debris. I put bills with bills. Contracts with contracts. I just saw it, she muttered. I know I did. She crumpled a flyer and tossed it into the trash. Hold on a second, I said. I retrieved the knot of paper from the bin, smoothed it flat: environmental-protection spam. Back on hands and knees, I reached beneath the sofa and found printouts of emails I had sent, mock-ups for the covers of her books. I'd tried to explain we didn't need to keep hard copies of emails, but here they were. The towel was slowly unwinding from the self-help author's head and falling toward the floor, revealing her loose red locks, dark and wet. The color would grow brighter as it dried, and then she'd really be aflame.

Ha!

Triumphant, she produced a pale blue slip and raised it into the air. Here it is.

Thanks, I said.

She stood, secured the towel. Then her gaze fell on the package, docked like an abandoned raft in the paper slough.

What did you order?

It was exactly the question I had in mind. I lifted the envelope, held it to my chest. It was book-shaped, I decided. Oh, just an encyclopedia, I said. Of poems. The self-help author stared at me another moment. Her cheeks were pink, as was the outline of her face, tinged with quiet dye. It's an Eastern European anthology, I said. Unabridged. Who knows how these improvisations came to mind? The self-help author was right: I wasn't usually so quick with lies, or at least omission was more my forte. She invited me to bring the anthology to the reading on Sunday, pop by with a bottle of wine. I agreed. I was in the stairs, I was at home, where Misha was in bed, asleep, before I remembered I'd gone to tell her just the opposite: that we wouldn't make it to the reading after all.

7

In the kitchenette, I plugged in the nest of holiday lights. Then I padded across the tiles and wrote a note, *Cancel poems!* and stuck it to the wall. There were other notes above the credenza: *Insta-Ad*; *Misha's presentation*; *sweet potatoes (??)*; *Psychic when?* They constituted a sort of telegraph station where Misha and I communicated back and forth, trying to connect. We overlapped for only a few hours in the early morning when he woke up, or in the evening when he came home, and so in the intervening day (or in my case, night) we scribbled annotations. Since I'd been gone, Misha had responded to one of mine: *yes potatoes (the purple ones?)*. There were a few older notes that repeated the same message again and again, reverberating across the wall. *Where did you go? Where did you go?* I still didn't know how to respond.

Beneath *Misha's presentation*, a question appeared.

you'll come?

I selected a pencil from the coffee mug.

of course.

I reread my response. It seemed to me terse.

of course!

Marriage, I thought, was quite possibly one long note to self, a work in progress constantly revised.

I wrote,

i wouldn't miss it for the world.

Then I sat at the credenza with the package and slit the sealed flap.

Inside was a book. As I'd imagined. I unsheathed it from the bubble wrap. It was an exhibition catalog, and the name of a familiar gallery was splashed across the front. The artist on view was also familiar. I felt my stomach drop, and for once the nebula was not to blame. I knew this artist rather well.

I'd almost married him, in fact.

I do not believe in serendipity. I don't think there are moments, of which so many people speak, in which a life irrevocably and neatly forks, like a line in your palm. I believe instead that the past returns to you in waves, crashing onto the shore, so that the ground on which you stand is always shifting, like a beach, imperceptibly renewed.

What I think is that New York is a small city, in the end, equipped with some strange gravity that is forever pulling you nearer those people you'd rather avoid: you're drawn back to the same places, the same games, ten years down the road. I was resigned, in other words, to the idea that my former fiancé and I would cross paths once again. I hadn't expected it to come about in quite this way. I ran a hand along the title page. There was his name, unmistakable, serifed and in all caps.

I looked around my apartment as if through a stranger's eyes. I had always considered my studio as a site of potential, a precursor to the sort of place in which I'd like to live. In this moment, however, it was simply a reflection of how things were. The walls were blank but for the notes, the shelves filled with Misha's findings from the beach, onion slices languished in a strainer in the sink—I stuck them in the fridge. The whole scope of my life could be taken in with a single glance. I opened the book to consider, by contrast, what my fiancé had achieved.

The catalog was hardcover—a serious book for a serious debut. One hundred thick and glossy pages, heavy with ink. Well, I thought. How swell for him. After all, not everyone had the gumption to become a photographer so late in his career. I glanced again at the picture on the cover, a little relieved to see it was beautiful but boring, something I'd seen before: a nude woman asleep on a bed. I wondered if she was the woman he was seeing now. She had nice knees, I thought. They were smooth and blended with her thighs. I would have traded a great deal for unobtrusive knees like hers. I made a quick calculation in my head. She would have to be a lot younger than he was, even younger than I had been, when my fiancé and I first met. He was no artist back then.

And yet—

THE EXHIBITION OF PERSEPHONE Q
SEPTEMBER 12, 2001–MARCH 15, 2002

A leaflet floated to the credenza when I cracked the spine. I held it to the holiday lights.

> *Disclaimer: After the tragedy of the towers, viewers will no doubt approach these photographs through a veil of mourning. While the artist could not have foreseen the events of 9/11, these works anticipate with uncanny clarity the loss of the towers as well as the many complicated questions that have followed. An extraordinary debut from one of New York's most promising photographers,* The Exhibition of Persephone Q *constitutes a profound exploration of privacy, memory, and the instability of truth . . .*

I set these explorations to the side.

I had not spoken to the provocateur in question for over a decade. Ours was a familiar story: he was older, and at the time I was too young, too malleable, in search of models for how to live. It was all so long ago, and I wouldn't say I had any particular resentment toward my fiancé now. I was glad for his success. Even still, one must always be suspicious of a superlative. There are many captivating debuts in this city—in any city—every year. Forays into the avant-garde. Much snubbing of tradition. New York is endlessly capable of swallowing them up. My fiancé, back when that's what he was to me, was a financier who spent his free time with a camera slung around his neck. I wasn't aware he'd had greater ambitions then.

I read:

> *Photographs are so often received as factual records of the past, but here the artist draws our attention to the fragility of historical narrative in an age when digital editing software will soon become a staple in the average American home . . .*

On the computer, geometric forms folded in on themselves, drifting between the borders of the screen. I looked at Misha, asleep in our bed. Were we another demographic staple, an average American home? I glanced again at the image on the title page and frowned. I wondered if it wasn't a little cheap to stake a debut on tragedy this way.

> *In these photographs, the disappearance of major landmarks, including the Chrysler and Empire State buildings, and, most notably, the towers, challenges received ideas about America's most recognizable skyline. The juxtaposition of these manipulated scenes suggests that any one of these variations might be the "original." The viewer wonders: Which is "authentic"? Which is "correct"?*

A blue night tunneled down the air shaft. The hum of a television filtered through the wall, not quite masking the sound of the psych student's retching as she expelled a very late lunch.

> *Though the world within the photographs grows increasingly menacing and strange, the woman on the bed seems unconcerned. The passage of historical time, recorded in the destruction of the city out the window and in the deterioration of the room, has no effect on her . . .*

This seemed a little unfair. She was asleep, after all. Who knows what she would have felt if she'd woken up?

Ten years ago, I suppose I understood ambition less. Naïveté was my only talent. Perhaps this was still the case—I had trouble remembering that not everyone's approach to life was quite the same as mine. People were after power, IRAs, two bedrooms and one-and-a-half baths. They worried about their children, fluoride levels, lead paint leaching into lungs. It never occurred to me to fear the water, the paint, the rest of the world, until it was too late, and I was already sick. When I was still with my fiancé, I was the one who had a claim to the arts, and he worked in a bank, structuring debt, which is to say he wasn't a photographer at all. He thought of things in terms of p's and q's, where p parameterizes the likelihood of success, q failure, such that $p + q = 1$. Tickets for shows arrived months in advance. *If we're still together, we should go . . .* I was curious and half in love, I waited around to see. I hadn't been in the city long, wasn't so long out of college. I was anxious to see how people lived. It mattered less to me what my fiancé's view on things was than that he had one: *If . . .* We went to the movies, to the river, dismantled paper dosas. He opened a bagel and passed me his lox. I was spending more and more time with him, soon enough I didn't have a bed of my own. *If we weren't together . . .* was a phrase I picked up all on my own, only after we were engaged. I lay awake at night, slightly stunned. I felt the rest of my life closing in, like a lake narrowing into a stream. I was twenty-three, curious in a way that ran counter to love. I suppose curiosity won.

I turned the page. I hoped he was happier now with this woman on the bed. The curators had a point—she looked very stationary indeed. Reliable. The mattress was an exponent of inertia. The light was low and flattering, highlighting her knees.

> *Who, after all, is Persephone Q?*
> —*The Curators*

I am slow to anger, fear, to recover purses stolen on the street or say the things I ought to say. Once, at Insta-Ad, I dropped a box of CDs on my bare foot from some height, and I stood there for a long moment, toes crushed, so transfixed by how a simple task could turn so utterly against me that the pain set in at an unaccountable delay. Ouch, I said. As a girl, in school, there was one year during which a very fine overcoat spent months on a hook by the classroom door. No one knew whose it was. It hung there solemnly through spring, until the faux-fur collar began to lose its shape, and it was only on the last day of school, when the classroom was empty, the walls stripped, that the coat took on an aura of familiarity. I lifted it from the hook, turned it around. My mother produced it from the closet for special occasions only. How could I not have noticed it was mine? So it was with the pictures. I'd been flipping through the book for nearly an hour before I realized. I looked at the woman. I looked at myself. Alone in the kitchen, I said it out loud.

Hey, I said. That's me.

It should not take so long to identify oneself.

And I'm afraid my capacity for self-recognition was even worse than that—I did not recall myself so much as I recalled the room. The walls were red. The sheets were white. The skyline asserted itself against the sky. The Chrysler Building was prim beneath its pearly crown. Ten years ago I too had fallen asleep to such a vantage. I was living in Brooklyn, by the river, where, out my window, on a very clear day, I had a Manhattan view. I imagined my fiancé standing in the doorway with his camera, the memory of an argument still fresh in his mind. On a coatrack in the corner hung a long silk robe, and there was no reason to think that it could not be mine. In fact I could feel it on my skin. I always felt fantastic in that robe. I was queen of my red room, in silk. And it dawned on me then that I, of course, was Persephone Q. That was my bed. My robe. My bright red room.

I flipped forward through the book. The same woman was on display over and over again, lying on the bed before the window. Her back, hips, thighs, and elbows were flush to the mattress. Her face was turned to the side. She'd fallen asleep looking across the river, just as, incidentally, I used to do. The eye traveled along the cliff of her jaw, the thick of the belly, the flat of the hips, the cunt. Nothing was left to the imagination except the woman's face . . . *The privacy of the scene positions the viewer in the role of "voyeur"* . . . The purview reached her neck, her chin, the lobe of an ear, then stopped. She turned her head away.

Stranger things were happening in the world of the frame. The same photograph was reproduced multiple times, as previewed in the exhibition text, except that in each iteration the room was emptier, as if someone were stealing the woman's belongings while she slept. Objects went missing: lamps, books, posters. Hooks came down from the walls. Furniture moved out, butterflies and moths moved in. Nature, it seemed, was winning. Moss crept along the baseboards at the edges of the room, and damp stains colonized the plastered red, deepening the walls to a sanguine maroon. Buildings disappeared outside the window, just as the curators had described. It was strange to see them go. There went the Chrysler Building, the Empire State. The towers. I felt a pang. Meanwhile, *The woman remains unchanged, suggesting two distinct timelines within the very same picture.* It was true. Through all of this, she lay alone in the soft white sheets, one limp arm extended, as if reaching for something on the floor. I sympathized. I, too, reached for things in sleep. I was known to scream and talk and laugh. It used to drive Misha mad. What's so funny? he said. What is so sad?

> *With her intelligent limbs and languid pose, the woman*
> *is unperturbed. Her prominence recalls ancient symbols of*

woman as mythic force, arbiter of nature's powers in civi-
lization's domain. And yet, she is subject to the male gaze.

I looked out the window. I looked at the book. I gazed at my intelligent limbs.

It slips away from you, your name. As a girl, I was Marie Antoinette, eating cake. I was tree-limbed Daphne in the woods with my dogs. In Spanish class at school, I was Lupita. In German, Wilhelmine. As an adult, I still felt startled when people said my name aloud. Misha called me Babe. With the self-help author, I was Doll. My fiancé had assigned so many endearments and diminutives that I felt like a whole collection of women bound into one, a composite of *-let*s and *-chen*s and *-kin*s, in addition to further derivatives and declensions I'd rather not remember here. Now he had renamed me once again. Persephone Q. For all intents and purposes, we were one and the same.

It was upsetting to think that my fiancé had held on to this picture. Perhaps it should have made me furious. And yet I looked so peaceful there, asleep, so very asleep that I looked dead. I rarely slept so well anymore. I looked more closely. There was a tenderness in the camera's approach. It struck a respectful distance that belied a longing, as in the photograph of a building you admire in a city that is not yours. I paused. I am no building, I thought. No attraction among the bombed-out boulevards of Warsaw, rebuilt as if nothing had happened there. I tried to coax forth a flame of spite. Only I was not furious. I hadn't known he'd looked at me this way.

I wondered what I would have written, had my fiancé's show come to me with a request for copy.

> . . . *intelligent limbs, re-gifting woman the voice that she has lost* . . .

Probably much the same.

One cannot blame the curators. I myself had been in this position once, writing texts for galleries and catalogs, prose that appeared on whitewashed walls as authorless as dew. At the art auction house where I worked when I was still with my fiancé, I sat at my desk and deferred to something like consensus truth, a voice that belonged to the museum itself. You might even say it came to me too naturally. The two women with whom I took lunch, by contrast, were subjectivity machines. They held very strong opinions about very specific things. At the deli, they specified (half spinach, half iceberg, feta, pepperoni, carrots, and dressing on the side). I was prone to ordering the number seven. They were complete and at ease in what seemed to me an uneasy world—they made the world conform to them. Over our midday salads, I listened as they planned the rest of their lives. One would work at the auction house for two or three more years to pay off her student loans before beginning an art consultancy of her own. Constance, top of her class, master's minted on scholarships, had no student debt, and she was busy forging contacts at MoMA and the Met. Both planned to have children between the ages of thirty-five and thirty-nine. They were women of considerable accomplishments and energies, capable of long-term commitments so correlative with individual success. As for me, I had no such hopes. I was going home to wash dishes, have sex. I had no idea what my life would look like in five years' time. The way my fiancé spoke of the future, it seemed as unpredictable as a living thing: *If we're still together . . .* I wondered, sometimes, as my colleagues composed their final forkfuls of salad, if I was missing some gland generative of the will to get ahead. Or perhaps I was simply too invested in staying behind.

I had half a mind to call these women and resurrect our lunchtime powwows. It struck me that they would know exactly what to do. They would have opinions on the ups and downs of love, the moral seriousness of pinching your husband's nose, forcibly holding his breath; advice on caffeine intake and midwives and Lamaze, whether or not a nebula can hear a symphony played on computer speakers pressed against the womb. They would know whether my fiancé deserved the extravagant praise the exhibition book lavished upon his debut show. But it had been ten years since I'd set foot in an office cubicle. I was sure these women, too, had quit.

It's hard not to believe a gallery wall. I could still hear the cadence of that voice, like a radio left on in my brain. There were a great many radios left on in my brain. *If, if . . .* To which should I be attuned? I had moved on from that life, as regular people do, by way of selective suppression of the truth. Though I suppose if elision is just another way to lie, then I was guilty of this, too.

My knives were still scattered across the table, blades fanned. I reached for one and placed the point to the spine of the book, drawing along the binding the way I had learned to section the membrane of an orange. A glossy page fell to the floor. I retrieved it. I sliced another page with care. It seemed like the logical thing to do. The holiday lights nested on the credenza, and I held the photographs to their weak light. Separated from the book, the pictures seemed benign. I admired the craftsmanship. I admired myself. I sliced another page and studied the severed image of the woman in her decaying room. For a moment it seemed she might be someone else. I was almost disappointed. She lay supine, breasts and belly profiled against the gray of the sky and the white of the bed. Flesh fell toward spine. She sank. I noticed the floral pattern of the pillow, the angle of the crooked lampshade by the bed—at least while the lamp was still there, before it was digitally ferried offstage. I looked for some sign of the small, reptilian scar that I carry like a stamp on my upper ribs, a vestige of the tubes that were once inserted to help me breathe when I was young. But the bedsheets rose so that you could not see. I was saddened to think that I could not recognize my body without the tattoo of the scar or some hint of my face. That I'd perennially underestimated my knees. I was no more qualified to identify myself, I thought, than any stranger might have been.

I did what one does in such a situation: I searched. Online, the pictures took an extremely long time to load. I typed in *("spouse" OR "girlfriend") AND* my fiancé's name. I tried *"Persephone Q" AND "who is the woman in."* Every query led me back to him. I was confused. The web was not wondering about the woman at all, despite the question the curators had posed. I searched *"contact" AND "telephone"* and found an email address. There were three, in fact. He could be reached via Yahoo, Earthlink, and AOL.

I spent the rest of the night composing a note, addressed it to the trinity, bcc:

> Remember me? I'm the American who looks a little Slavic. Ha.
>
> It's occurred to me I maybe look more American than I used to. Anyway.
>
> I'm sorry it's been so long. I owe you a whole decade of Happy Birthdays: Happy Birthday, times ten!
>
> And congratulations! What a surprise to receive the exhibition catalog. Although I couldn't help but notice that you didn't tell me about these pictures before. Maybe because you didn't have my number? Or my name? Well, it's right here, below, so maybe now you can add it.
>
> Here it is,
>
> Percy

When I finished, I stood for a moment in the center of the room. The apartment was as still as it had been the night my mother's serving bowl fell from the shelf, and I was more exhausted than I had been in days. I padded to the bed, where Misha was sound asleep. I watched his breath rising and falling in the sheets. I wished very much to wake him. I reached—then pulled away. For the first time since I had pinched his nose, I lifted the blankets and slipped in beside him. Folding my arms firmly across my chest, I composed myself a simple lullaby: I will not harm, I will not harm. I lay awake for what seemed like hours, vigilant.

8

I woke up in a terror and looked at my hands. Who knows what they'd been up to while I slept, but I was glad to find them empty now, and that I was alone in the bed. I fell back into the sheets, relieved.

Outside, it was still dark. I could hear Misha in the bath, washing his face. The same sounds as every morning drifted into the room: the little gulp he made when he cupped his hands and splashed away the soap. He emerged, zipped into multiple layers of down to protect against the Atlantic spray.

You're awake.

I guess so.

He looked down at his wool socks.

Do you want to come?

Maybe not today.

Misha slid four slices of rye into the toaster. I watched the wires orange. Out the window, in the air shaft, a fine powder glimmered. The first snow! It was almost enough to make me change my mind about accompanying my husband to the Rockaways. That I never went to comb the sands with him was a source of guilt. Then I saw it wasn't snow at all, but a fine trail of flour. The white bag soon followed, drifting to the square of cement below.

Misha, what if we moved to California?

He nicked idly at the butter with a knife more appropriate for deboning chicken thighs.

Think of the beaches, I said.

He shrugged.

I cannot drive.

Many people, recently, had thought of moving away. They pointed to security alerts of yellow and red and orange. The anthrax. The attacks. My reaction had always been the opposite: The threat was out there, so we ought to stay in, stay put. Look at the data, I said. We're over-due for war. Look at the data, Misha replied. You are almost always safe. Meanwhile, probabilities hovered over Times Square like smog. I remembered the sirens, the radios, the commotion down the hall when the internet news stuttered, then crashed, as the second tower brought it down. I'd gone downstairs to borrow the self-help author's phone and found her cradling an armful of thorns: she'd gathered all the cacti from the window boxes, as if to protect them from the fumes. I dialed Misha to no avail. *Hello, you've reached Insta-Ad* . . . It would be just like him to take a downtown detour on a weekday whim. He was too curious, too receptive, too accommodating of a world out to take advantage of him. Then he was there, at the door. He'd walked sixty blocks. His bed at Insta-Ad was far away, separated from the city by sawhorse barriers and the strobe lights of police cars. For days we lay on the floor upstairs, listening to our Discmans. The apartment was mine, soon enough it was ours. Misha never really left.

The toaster chimed. He fished in the baskets with a fork—the ejection pedal had lost its leverage long ago. He retrieved a slice, wrapped it in a napkin, and slipped this, like a ticket, into the pocket of his coat.

Misha, I said. You'll burn your hand.

He kissed my forehead.

I'll see you at noon, he said.

That morning, I tried hard not to think about the exhibition. It took some work. I walked Misha to the train. On the way home, I bought potatoes, selecting the tubers carefully, one by one. I took my time. There were no blue ones. I chose the red. I paid the vendor exactly, counting out the change.

When I was back inside, it was only 6:00 a.m. I took out the trash, separating waxy cartons from the cardboard in Harold's honor. I did our delicates and hung them on the roof to dry. I took a bath. Vomited. Washed again. Then I gathered the self-help author's most recent manuscript at the credenza and stared dumbly at the lines.

Sometimes there is doubt that the other person is right for you.

I crossed out "sometimes" and considered the sentence again.

There is doubt . . .

Stylistically speaking, I thought the declarative had a pleasing ring. The self-help author wasn't given to certitude, however. That wasn't what self-help was about. Ours was an ongoing duel in which she added qualifications and I pared them away.

I restored the sentence and read it again.

Sometimes there is doubt . . .

Then I leaned back in the chair and peered into the air shaft, where the super was sweeping at the flour, drawing damp clouds from the cement. I watched his shoulders swaying in his blue jumpsuit.

The computer awoke with a chime.

It was only prudent, I reasoned, to keep myself apprised of the exhibition. I had almost married the artist, after all, and who knew what sort of thing might appear on his home page. In a new "tab," I typed in my fiancé's name. I scrolled. The links were worn, faded to the purple of a bruise. I simply clicked again. *Controversial . . .* his bio read. The same opinions proliferated, diverged, split hairs in the *Journal*, the *Voice*, the *Times*, where critics argued over the political implications of the show. Its genius and impetuousness. *A major artist . . .* important people mused. They had reservations about the depiction of the dwindling skyline. They'd accused the artist of *misogyny* and *pigheadedness*. I paused. Was that correct? I myself had been billed as a misogynist before. I'd internalized too much, the self-help author said, of the logic of the world. I remember I'd consulted Harold, as I often did when I needed to break a tie. He stood in his door, gave me one of his shrugs. Sorry, Percy. Not my area of expertise.

I searched *("girlfriend" OR "spouse") AND ("lawsuit" W/5 "art")*. I typed in my own name and met familiar friends. The librarian. The scientist. The porn star, who'd recently won an industry award. I found my way to the gallery website, which spewed superlatives recycled from the catalog. A particularly salacious photo flickered into being. I squinted at the half-loaded picture. I tried to greet it as a stranger might. This could be any woman on the bed, in any woman's room. She was a site of exegesis, as anonymous as ruins. Wasn't it better if no one knew her origins? Of course, I thought, it was only a matter of time before everything would be revealed. People would start talking and then they wouldn't stop. Soon everyone would know: I was Persephone Q. And vice versa, I supposed.

I checked my inbox again.

Nothing new save a chain letter from Yvette.

   Sorry, I'm a sucker for these . . .

―――――

I hobbled to the bath. At ten weeks, the nebula drew forth waves of nausea like a moon, regular as tides. We were a chorus of retching, the psych student and I. Back in the kitchenette, I secured in my palm a tuft of steel wool. With renewed energy, I attacked the burners on the stove.

My mother was a heroic housekeeper, at least when the mood to keep house struck. You didn't exist to her when she was cleaning the stove. The whole world fell away, and perhaps it was not too late to inherit this quality myself. At least until noon. I opened the oven door and laid siege to the grates. I tried to remember when I'd last cleaned them. Maybe I never had. The steel chipped away at char. I came up for air. As I scoured an old soup pot in which I had never made a soup, my thoughts incorporated, materialized before me like further appliances in need of cleaning. I addressed them one by one.

This would not be the first time my fiancé had announced major news through the mail. He had to have been the one to send the catalog. And yet, the exhibition had been open for months. Why not forward it along at once? As I scrubbed, I recalled the year my fiancé and I fell apart. There was a terrible fight, or at least I think there was, and I went uptown, to Morningside, to sign a sublease on an apartment of my own—the very apartment in which I still live—a whole hour's walk away. It was the easiest move I ever made. There were no movers, no guarantors. I arrived with little more than a duffel and a change of shoes. Most of what I owned I'd left behind with him. I went to work, came home, undressed, ate a sandwich at the sink. I had three or four outfits with me, a toaster, a stack of books. *The Diary of a Nobody*, though it made me sad, *On Murder Considered as One of the Fine Arts*, by Monsieur De Quincey, and *An Essay on the Noble Science of Self-Justification*. I was especially partial to the Edgeworth. I slept on a mattress on the floor. I'd have to go back eventually to retrieve my things, and I assumed I'd simply stay. Meanwhile I enjoyed being alone, knowing I'd wind up back with my fiancé. Then, one afternoon, an envelope arrived. The address bore his clear, neat script. I opened the seal in the hall, and a key tumbled into my palm. The fob bore the logo of a storage facility downtown. He'd packed everything I owned and locked it away. There would be no reconciliation after all.

I sprayed more cleaning fluid, coughed. I consulted the label on the bottle. There were no warnings for pregnant women that I could see. I closed the broiler drawer. The plastic crisper slid easily from the fridge, and I lowered it into the sink. Suds splashed across the counter and slid onto the floor.

As I rinsed and dried the refrigerator shelves, I considered a second and more alarming possibility: my fiancé had nothing to do with the package at all. Ten years down the road, he might not care to let me know about his recent success. I wouldn't have been surprised if he'd forgotten about me altogether, lost track of crucial information. Like my name. After all, this was a man who'd neglected his own save-the-date, RSVPing, incredibly, to a different wedding held the very same day as ours. We're flexible, he said. I had always regarded these gaffes with a kind of wonder. But who else would have sent it, if not he? I ruled myself out—I was never so dazed and delirious as that. I considered the self-help author. My psychic. Even Harold crossed my mind. I thought of the random number generator at Insta-Ad, still on the fritz, the matching algorithms meant to pair consumers with banner ads. Perhaps they were more powerful than I'd thought.

I peered into the air shaft, where the super was still sweeping. He looked up at the column of windows that rose above his head. With a jolt, I stepped away. I scolded myself. Look how paranoid you're becoming. Nothing's even happened yet.

A roach skittered out from beneath the broiler, a big grandfather roach, like a buckeye with legs. Hi, friend, I said. Then I glanced at the clock. Ten. It struck me my psychic was exactly the person to ask about such extraordinary events. In the mirror in the hall, I applied some blush. I dropped my keys into my purse. Then I was in the lobby, I was out on the street. It was only as the building door, freshly restored with tinted glass, closed behind me that I felt the first twinge. He couldn't have forgotten. And yet, in all those interviews and exhibition texts, he hadn't once thought to mention me.

9

My psychic was not a morning person. Nevertheless, I stood beneath the red awning outside her storefront and rang the buzzer with my usual persistence. After a few minutes, she appeared. Ugh, she said. Her eyes were swollen, and a stray charm clung like a beetle to her hair. She rubbed her face. Percy, she said. Come in.

Sometimes, when I went to visit my psychic, it seemed that she was the one who needed to talk. Such was the case today. I followed her inside and settled on a pouf. Percy, Percy, she said, as she plugged in a hot plate, set the kettle for tea. The heavens can be a bitch. She ran the flat of her palm along a temple. A formidable bitch indeed. But other times, mind you, fate manifests in the form of man. She produced a sachet of chamomile from the roomy sleeve of her robe and dunked it into her empty mug. The velvet drapes, drawn snugly around the storefront, were a bulwark against the day, and in the resultant dim I could hardly see her face. She seemed so fragile that morning, shielding her eyes. I don't know how much longer I'll last, she said. My landlord's driven the rent up again. That's awful, I replied. She pushed a palm against the dark, as if bad luck were as easily deflected as a ray of light. Oh, I'll fight it, she said. Just you watch. He's been trying to have me out for years, but I persevere. Urban renewal is a fuck in the ass. Excuse me, Percy. But it's the truth. It's us small business owners who get screwed. I nodded. There were plans for a megamall on 125th, and already banners had begun to eclipse the old marquees. I hate Old Navy, I

"The American consumer is a casual consumer."

Misha studied the floor.

I think I will wear at least the shoes, he said.

The following week, Misha was to speak at an annual start-up expo, a carnival of poster boards and booths and gratis stress balls held in a warehouse near Port Authority that I had thought was meant for storing cars. Normally it was Misha's advisor who appealed to investors, but these days venture capitalists sought younger talent. Ivy League grad, Bulgarian accent? They couldn't say no to Misha, his advisor said. I agreed. He was commanding in his tweed. He paced as he talked, uncapping and recapping a marker with his thumb. I was a one-woman audience in the window, taking notes.

Everyone is afraid of how consumers will respond when they learn their data is being stored and auctioned. But what if you encrypted cookies? Insta-Ad is making consumer data safer than ever—

I raised my hand.

Isn't the whole point how much more attractive online shopping becomes?

We went through the entire presentation slide by slide. It was a real dress rehearsal. He walked me through the company valuation as if I were an investor. I nodded along, pushing the self-help author's thoughts on role-play from my mind. In the start-up business money moved like water, I was learning. Cash flowed. Accountants churned. Fresh funds poured into reservoirs set aside for droughts. In a healthy firm, revenues parted around unforeseen obstacles, like a stream around a rock. Misha laser-pointed at images projected onto the wall. As you can see, he said, the burn rate is high, but comparable to endeavors of similar size. I studied the corresponding graph, where many lines traversed a downward trend. He ran a thin hand through his hair. His widow's peak was sharpening, drawing inward at the sides.

I had every confidence in Misha's talents. It seemed there was no problem he could not solve. How he and his advisor planned to transform those solutions into income, however, was something I did not quite grasp. Not that I myself possessed much pecuniary sense. My own finances were plenty unreliable. I took pleasure in the pale blue envelopes that arrived at my door from various origins, checks that could be summed every which way to make the rent. For most of my life I had lived like this, converting piles of mail into cash. It was not a very profitable endeavor. It's possible I should have worked a little more. Certainly I *could* have worked a little more. I ought to have found a more regular and better-paying job, especially now that the nebula was on its way. As matters stood, I had not. I'd done the mental math. Plus child. Minus rent. The margins were suboptimal, and yet I was not moved to action. There was only the mood I was in today, and hunger, nausea, more work to do tomorrow, which was how I'd fallen into the habit of eating rice, peanut butter, and other no-chop foods, soy sauce packets stolen on the sly. The projector shone with lunar clarity on Misha's skull where his hairline had begun to retreat. I was wrong about many things, and I hoped Insta-Ad's prospects were among them.

Perhaps it really was the future of online shopping, of all shopping, and Misha would no longer need to worry. He'd keep his hair. Though he seemed to want nothing to do with the fruits of his own labor. He regarded his algorithms with a kind of paternal disgust. He often said when he came home, Honestly, I am not feeling good about this at all.

An easel stood before a mini-fridge stocked with cucumbers and coffee. Misha took up a length of fresh white chalk and began to section the board. He labeled one half "cookies." On the other, he wrote "bids." These being determined by criteria advertisers give beforehand, he said. A client might ask to target traders who telemark ski and live in New York. And how might a firm like Insta-Ad corral such a population? Cookies, of course. Misha divided the cookies column into a grid and labeled every section. Username. Location. Occupation. IP address. One rectangle flowed into the next. The diagram recalled an engine, only this one was silent, devouring data, not gas. What we have in the end, Misha said, is a cookie match. He connected the cookie-flow to the bid-flow and in the center hashed an asterisk. *A match.* What Insta-Ad did best, he explained, was to maintain efficiency while preserving anonymity, as ads and consumers were wedded in real time. The projector flung the advantages over industry competitors onto the opposite wall.

> Privacy-protected!
>
> Real-time matches!
>
> Superior bidding logic!
>
> Encrypted!

I raised my hand again.

Do you need all those exclamation marks?

Misha stood back and studied the wall.

Probably not, he said.

He went to the computer and tapped a few keys. On the wall, the exclamation marks disappeared one by one. Then he joined me in the window, sliding the pot of African violets to the side. I looked across the room at the diagram he had made. Arrows spawned and darted, connecting names with addresses and number of clicks, the binary variable (if purchase, then 1; else 0) that recorded whether or not the consumer had bought what she'd been told to buy. The scent of hamburger and curry carried from the street. I picked at the loose threads that rose, like a halo, from the worn tweed of Misha's jacket. Beneath my palm, I felt him heave and sigh.

You did great, I said.

I reached out to comfort him, placed a palm on his cheek. How very tired he seemed, even though, from my perspective, he was nearly always asleep. The folds beneath his lids were lilac. I missed him. I pressed his shoulder. Hey. His collarbone. Hey. I pressed hard. He swayed. I watched my hand pass over his face and come to rest on his chin. Wake up, I said. Then my fingers floated to his nose. I pinched it softly. Misha looked at me. A glimmer wavered in his eyes like a cursor on a screen. He reached out and took my nose in turn. Touché. We sat there, holding on. Let's have a hold-your-breath contest, I suggested. Misha shook his head, tugging my wrist to and fro. Then he shrugged. All right. He gulped the air and pursed his lips. I puffed my cheeks. We looked at each other, eyes wide. Outside, two people called to one another on the street. A car passed, and its music swelled and faded. I counted backward in my head as my lungs began to burn. The stopper in my diaphragm was knocking at my chest. I gasped. Misha's fingers released, my own hand fell away. He smiled, his cheeks only slightly flushed. I guess I win, he said. We looked across the room. The flowchart of the bidding logic tangled on the board.

We went for coffee, returned, rehearsed some more. Further exclamation marks were trimmed, and Misha was able to appear less obviously bored when discussing financial trends. Then it was dark. The radiator had quieted hours ago, and the room was chilled. Misha switched off the projector, closed the windows. He gathered the metal detecting wand, his Walkman, my hand. Together, we descended the stairs and emerged onto the street, where Misha fitted headphones over his ears. I did the same. It was that sort of night, that sort of mood, when we were in need of Brahms. We walked in silence. I wished that it would snow. We passed the Turkish baths. The doors opened, and bathers emerged. Eucalyptus billowed down the street. Lanterns splashed the walkways in Washington Square. Misha gripped my bare fingers in his gloves. He gave my hand a squeeze. I felt so close to him, and also a little afraid.

I spent the night in sleepless deliberation, wandering the streets. By the time I reached home, it was Tuesday, and I'd come to a decision: I'd visit the gallery after all, see the pictures for myself. Just once. Then I'd set this whole business of the exhibition aside.

That morning, after Misha left, his pockets full of toast, I dressed carefully, sliding hangers to the side until I found a blouse I hadn't worn in years. The stiff white bib hung like a dried flower in the sheath of the dry-cleaning bag. I reached for the shelf above and found a yellow silk scarf with a smattering of daisies. Why not? I draped it over my shoulders. When I was finished, I studied my reflection in the mirror. The blouse puffed up with shoulder pads. The silk scarf shone. I had almost masked the nervousness I felt.

I checked my email. No messages. I replied-all to my fiancé's triumvirate:

> Just wondering if you got my message!
>
> Main question again is why you never told me about the pictures?
>
> A response would be nice.
>
> Thanks!

By the way this is Percy.

(Again.)

Percy Q.

Outside, on the street, couples filled the windows of every café, and this tableau, multiplied across storefronts, applied itself to lowering my mood. They nursed glasses of orange juice and mugs of coffee, gazed sleepily at plates of buttered rolls and hollandaise. A man in a window, his fork poised over a plateful of eggs, glanced my way, and I felt a loose seam within me zip. Then I looked over my shoulder and caught a glimpse of a beautiful woman in a cornflower coat disappearing into a marble lobby. I felt myself moving in parallel worlds, two lives, one in which I was always on view, the other in which no one thought to look twice.

The train platform was filled with high-spirited people. I followed them onto the downtown car. On baby-blue seats, I listened to the music others streamed through headphones. None of it was Brahms. A child began to cry, and I wondered at its desperation. My stop arrived. I threaded toggles through my pink trench and emerged onto postindustrial Chelsea streets that I had long avoided. Things had changed. A small park claimed a corner. The warehouses had been made over and fitted with glass, and in reflection, people loitered. I paused to pay my respects at a small and makeshift shrine: flyers of the missing, pasted to the brick. In the photos, they posed at weddings and graduations, blew wishes at birthday cakes. A laminated Post-it rose above the array like an exhibit label: *I never met you but I miss you*. There were a number of these impromptu memorials, and the city was quietly disappearing them, citing public safety: the damp papers released, like slick sighs, to the streets, bringing pedestrians down. I took a cold sip of air. I thought of my psychic, how she had reached for me, and felt the same tightness in my throat. Then I walked on, down abandoned blocks, drawing nearer to the river. I walked until there was no one around and stood outside the tall glass doors, a little surprised that I wasn't immediately recognized.

Inside, the gallery was open and white and silent, and I was the only viewer there. A brochure holder was fixed to the wall. I slipped a pamphlet from the stack. The glossy paper crackled . . . *a provocative show that arrives a little too late, or perhaps too soon* . . . I stuffed it into my purse. A woman behind a white enamel desk glanced at me. She said, encouragingly, Go on in. Then I felt obliged.

It is common knowledge how mutable a picture can be. An artwork changes with the light, the setting, the time and place. Would we look twice at Campbell's soup cans, I wonder, if they debuted above a mantel in a living room? Similar transformations occur, of course, when moving from your pantry into a gallery. Which is to say that nothing could have prepared me to see the photographs on such a scale. They were supersized. Leviathan. Enlarged beyond what one would ever willingly inflict upon an image of oneself.

What a difference simply zooming in can make! I had missed these dimensions while slicing through the catalog. The frames were blown up to the billboard proportions of a Pollock and hung regularly as windows on the walls. The scale made the viewer feel small. I took a slow turn around the gallery. Windows onto windows—I fell through. The red room was sparsely furnished: a coat stand, a chair, a bed with a ribbon tied to a post. I did love a ribbon, I couldn't ever bring myself to throw one away. Even today, when I receive a gift, a box of chocolates, a bouquet, I tie the ribbon to a doorknob or a post. And he was always buying flowers, I recalled. Sometimes for me. Sometimes for himself. I stood to the side of the picture and looked into the photograph from an angle, crouching to re-create more accurately the pillow-talk perspective from which I used to admire a very similar view. The Chrysler Building was distinct, it rose just so above the sill. I remembered it like a personal moon.

I had not loved that room when I was living there. I never love where I am, I would always rather be somewhere else. Now I missed those days when all my furniture was borrowed and the walls were red. How peaceful I looked, blown up, diffuse. Although it was rather public. I looked around the empty gallery. The receptionist was watching me from the corner of her eye. I placed a palm on my belly, below my ribs, and took long, deep breaths, quelling the midmorning nausea climbing up my spine.

Two women entered from the street. I turned with a jolt. They arrived in a flurry of sighs and adjustments and unbuttonings of coats, had similar movements and manners and hair that swooped and grayed. A mother and daughter, I thought, out for a walk.

I wondered if they'd recognize me in tandem, the same way they rearranged their scarves, shed gloves. The daughter dived into brochures while her mother tapped across cement, leaning heavily on her walker. I watched her peer through her glasses at my body. She stared for a long while, as if the fact of me did not compute. I knew the feeling. She was looking into the final frame, in which I lay naked and alone in an empty room, below an empty window. Only the stars had been spared deletion. She clucked her disapproval. Her daughter rolled her eyes.

Mum, she said. It's art.

I wondered what was taking them so long. Hey, I felt like shouting. That's me! The daughter, for her part, ignored me completely. She wended through the room, wool overcoat folded neatly in her arms. I followed. I wanted to track her expressions. I wanted to be seen. Perhaps I stood too close—I held my breath when she caught my eye. I could have sworn a flash of recognition crossed her face. She looked at me as if I were someone she had known in the distant past. Then she glanced back at the photographs. I felt a little shock, as if I'd won a raffle. I was about to say something corroborating, such as I could hardly believe it myself. Then she turned on a heel and rejoined her mum. I watched her whisper something into the old woman's ear.

What?

12

Once, in the eighties, a famous sculptor threw his much younger girlfriend, another artist, up-and-coming and Cuban-born, from the thirty-fourth-story window of the apartment they shared on Mercer Street. Ana Mendieta landed on a deli roof like a kind of human bomb. Perhaps the sculptor was afraid, as some men are, that she would consume his art. His sense of self. Or perhaps, as he testified, they were simply drunk and careless with their lives: she slipped. Although, no matter how drunk the husband, how does a woman slip up and out a window so surreptitiously he hardly notices? The poor man, said all the sculptor's friends, following his swift acquittal. He was made a scapegoat by the feminist mob. I knew of the affair in part because for years his work had sold at a premium. Everyone wanted to own a piece of a murderer's mind. As for my fiancé's show, beyond the fact that in the photographs I looked a little dead, a little dumb, the pictures carried no trace of violence. It wasn't apparent he'd done anything wrong. I found it confusing, really, that critics had expressed any interest at all.

In all my experience of art, I could find no precedent for how to proceed. I might not have proceeded. One thing I had learned from the self-help author, however, is that from time to time a woman must take matters of publicity into her own hands. I would be the first to break the news: I was Persephone Q. I was curious, too, about my fiancé's motives. Why, when he could have chosen any-one, any woman at all, had he used a picture of me?

In the back of my mind, there lurked the promise I had made to myself to set the exhibition aside. I meant to. But matters of aesthetic integrity were now at stake. The choice to present an ordinary woman in such gargantuan proportions struck me as artistically and exegetically significant. That the body lying on the bed was a real person the artist had known, an average citizen who buys her potatoes in the street, completely altered the interpretation spouted by the text on the wall. Was not a tension introduced, if the woman was mythically enlarged and at the same time everyday? Also, what did it mean to erase a lover from your past, elide both her belongings and her name? The hermeneutics went on and on. It was valuable, in the end, for me to come forth. A good gallerist could sell such a richly layered composition for upwards of ten thousand a piece, in which case there would soon be hundreds of thousands of dollars hanging on the walls. They might even sell one to the daughter here, who was at that very moment taking down the titles in a little notebook. *Untitled 1*, *Untitled 2*. I was no untitled. And yet, if a percentage of such a sale were to come my way, well—those were my belongings he was digitally expunging, after all.

I approached the reception area fully confident that my omission from the exhibition could be rectified efficiently, cordially, no trouble at all. It must have been an innocent mistake. My fiancé, absentminded as ever, would simply have forgotten to fill in some form. To fill me in on his art. An image of Claire, in her violet windbreaker, dashed through my mind, and I watched her go. I applauded myself on my neutral, placid manner, when, by most

accounts, it would have been perfectly acceptable to indulge in a little
angst. At the enamel enclave of the reception, a flurry of orchids rose
from a vase, extending a subtle canopy over the desk. The blooms
swayed softly as I cleared my throat. The receptionist looked up.

How can I help?

That woman in the photographs in there. She's me.

Who?

Me.

She leaned forward in her chair, looking past my ear and into
the gallery.

I'm afraid that's not possible.

Oh, it is, I said.

I told her about the Chrysler Building, the ribbon, my view. I'd lived
in that very room, I explained, the year before I moved in with my
fiancé, a decade ago. He would have taken the picture then. And by
the way, who better qualified to identify myself than me? You see
what I mean, I said. The receptionist began to rearrange the papers
on her desk, though I was fairly certain they were already in order.

Thank you for your concern.

You're welcome.

I waited. I cleared my throat.

So, what do you propose we do?

Her face was blank. The pendulums of her earrings swung.

Maybe if you referred me to the artist himself . . . ?

She thought for a moment.

No, I don't think so.

I stood beneath the orchids as she explained. She walked me through the latticework of relative liability, how I was a liability they were not liable to take on. How it was against gallery policy to become involved in personal disputes.

But this isn't personal. I am Persephone Q.

That really isn't possible.

Why not?

It just isn't the sort of thing the artist would do.

I spent every night looking at that view.

She gave me a weary look.

Honey, those pictures have nothing to do with you.

I was not the first one, she suggested, to react so strongly to a show. For this reason, it was protocol to refrain from sharing artists' personal information with visitors and fans. Like yourself, she said. The staff was likewise not responsible for the models their artists employed. Except I'd never been paid, that was the whole point. This was a candid, private photograph. And it happened to be of me. Given the pace of media of late, news would surely travel. She knew how it was. I wondered what I should say when people came asking about the show, and how I felt about appearing in it. I stood at her desk, palms pressed to the enamel. I considered stripping right there in the lobby, for proof, but it struck me as not worth the effort. I was wearing a lot of layers, after all. And she was no connoisseur.

Why would I lie?

The receptionist shrugged.

People say anything these days.

———

I have to say, I was impressed. When I was working at the auction house, we prided ourselves on our visual and historical intelligence, cultivated capacious memories for facts; the information was forever at our fingertips. Office lunches erupted in debates for or against the influence of Caravaggio on Rothko, whether Surrealism was the beginning of the end. Personally, I was a defender of the Dadaists. My lunch mate, Constance, was an office star. She had a genius memory for art, had famously rescued a Dutch Renaissance work that had been misattributed before it came through our doors. The receptionist at the gallery, by contrast, didn't seem nearly as sharp. And yet she was behaving as if I were the ignorant one. That was rather clever, I supposed. I reached out to touch an orchid petal, something real and benign. She grasped the vase with both hands and lugged it an arm's length away. I looked at her. Her oval ivory face and hair that shone like wax. I felt sorry for her, really. She was a bit of an orchid herself, pretty, delicate, aloof. Decidedly out of reach. I had no doubt that this was the sort of thing the artist would do. This was my fiancé par excellence, and I was the woman on the bed.

The mother and daughter had by this point joined us in the lobby, drawn by our debate. They loitered, pretending not to listen. But since of course they were eavesdropping, I turned to them. The woman in the photographs, I said. Can't you see that she is me? They blinked. The daughter rested the notepad against her chest in a gesture of mild shock. The old woman widened her eyes, and her thick glasses magnified them further still, revealing the pale blue of washed-out skies. That's my old room, I said. I used to live there. That's my bed, that's me. Do you really think I'd forget? The lobby was very silent. All three women stared. I felt betrayed. The receptionist coughed politely. She took a few deep breaths, as if this were all very distressing, poor for her health, though she couldn't have been more than twenty-five. She announced that she would happily bring my complaints to the attention of the curators and the artist himself. And I was quite free to go to the press. That was my right. Meanwhile, I could have her card. She rose to present it over the precipitous edge of the desk. Her voice, soft and low, struck a lullaby note meant to placate those who might erupt at any moment. Only I don't get angry with stupid people, I haven't the energy for that. As I turned to go, she pressed into my hands yet another exhibition book.

Here, she said. Have one of these on us.

13

I'm afraid my exit was less than alliance-forming. I turned on a heel and retraced my steps, past the victims' shrine and the park and the newly planted trees, the trunks nestled tenderly in mulch. Outside an old warehouse, a rat scurried into the street. It looked around, then retreated behind a rubble heap.

I walked without aim or end in mind, as if walking itself might lead me to some new world of unanimous accord. Instead I arrived at NYU. In Washington Square, the fountain sprayed. A cello player was performing beneath the arch, scales scooping along the stone. The sun had emerged, and the benches were draped with people who seemed to me without worry. They rewrapped scarves, discarded coffees, covered one another's mouths with mittens, stifling screams. I crossed the lawn to the law library, where, by way of an expired ID for an affiliate medical school (Yvette's), I gained entry to the stacks. The grotto of the basement reading room was cool and dark. I sank into a carrel behind the polished walnut shelves and set to work in search of legal precedent.

It is characteristic, maybe, for women of my age, of this era, to cram ourselves with information. To overprepare. To search until the evidence mounts in favor of what one already believes, in order that one may believe it. I read art historical decisions on the definition of fine art. I studied suits lodged by unwilling extras who'd appeared in movies they'd gone to see in theaters, not expecting to see themselves. Most of what I found, however, stood in defense of the artist's right to make his art regardless of opposition. At long tables with low lamps, the city's future crop of public defenders, corporate lawyers, counselors of every sort hunched over legal dictionaries, parsing court opinion. I wished one of them might litigate my mind, because the annals of *Questioning Aesthetics, Quarterly* certainly could not. The longer I was away from the gallery, the less sure I was of what I'd seen. It seemed almost possible I'd made a mistake. And yet. To misidentify myself—not even I was capable of so gross an oversight.

There were no windows in the basement reading room. Who knows how many hours passed? The law students rotated. They opened and closed their tomes, left, others took their places. I remained until I'd read myself into the company of peers.

There is a long tradition, of course, of artist-model symbiosis. For centuries painters have been falling for their models, marrying their models, replacing their wives with mistresses-as-models. It was always complicated, and the models rarely won. I read of Schiele's Wally and the wife he later married, for money; of Leonardo's model-pupil Salai, whom the genius sculptor kept like a pet in his home, a boy to be reproduced in bronze and plaster and marble until he died, three decades later, at the tender age of forty-four. Then there were the cases of Rembrandt and Saskia, his model-wife, and after her the servant girl Hendrickje—it was painting her that led him to propose. And of course there was Picasso, always Picasso, I perused whole diaries of his affairs. Olgas, Doras, Jackies. Round, beautiful women with doorstops for names. And I couldn't help but notice that when I compared the photographs of these women to the paintings in which they appeared, they almost never resembled themselves. They were either much improved, like Wally, or else their natural homeliness was exaggerated, as with Matisse's Marguerite. The lover's perspective transformed her. She was no longer the woman that she herself, glancing into the mirror behind the easel, would expect to see. Of course she wasn't. I could have laughed, I felt so relieved. I gathered the relevant copies of *The American Journal of Transdisciplinary Legal Aesthetics* into a stack and shoved them beneath my blouse, obscuring the bulk with pink trench and purse. I held them close on the train.

At home, the apartment was dark and Misha was asleep. I unloaded the journals onto the credenza, reached into the teapot for a handful of saltines. On the computer, there was a message waiting for me. It was from my fiancé.

> Dear Percy,
>
> Sorry, but I don't usually take pictures of Americans.
>
> Luck to you—

This performance of amnesia disarmed me to my seat. I reread the message until the words began to blur. I went straight to the teapot for more saltines.

14

I do not know how many days passed between the arrival of my fiancé's email and my eventual reply, but I can say it was at least one, and that it was spent primarily in bed, composing mental drafts. I rose occasionally for handfuls of saltines. I cleaned and cooked. No, I thought, munching crackers in the stairwell, I was not crazy. I was certain. Though I suppose self-assurance was no defense. In fact, it strengthened the charge.

Through Friday, whenever Misha left for Insta-Ad, I settled at the credenza to make my inquiries. I was always disappointed. The curators at the gallery did not return my calls. I only ever reached the voice mail. Hello, this is the woman featured in *The Exhibition of Persephone Q?* I'm calling to say, well, she is me. Or I am she. I paused. Anyway, I'm calling to express my disappointment, I said, that no one let me know. I recited my own number. Once, twice. I articulated every digit, crisp and clear. I look forward to your response, I said. I returned the phone to its lilac cradle. No one called me back.

Photography and I have never been a match. It was a primal and instinctive impulse, for me, to turn away from the lens. Whenever a camera emerged, I edged out of the frame. I hid my face. In my hands, in my lap, behind a book, behind a sudden interest in something over my shoulder, far away. Family albums feature ample studies of the back of my head. After that day in the gallery, however, I found that my feelings about being seen and photographed had changed. Documentation took on new meaning for me. My breasts were strange. My ankles swelled. I was exhausted all the time. On my nightly ramble, after dark, my mind chock-full of women—Doras, Wallys, Persephones—I slipped my hands into my pockets and felt the slight swell of my belly through the silk lining of my coat. Soon I'd stretch around four, six, nine months of life, and then I really wouldn't be the same. My bones would condense into the thick gray ash that fills an urn. This fate unfurled itself like a red carpet through the center aisle of my mind. I felt as though I might as well insist on my existential imprint while I still could.

One afternoon, I decided to call the women I used to work with at the art auction house. It seemed important not to use my own phone, in case the gallerists had shared my carefully articulated number with other people I might call, so I was at the self-help author's when I dialed, going over proofs. It was late afternoon, and she had just stepped out to clear her head. This was usually how the editing process went. We worked until one of us wandered off. Or until the self-help author wandered off, while I stayed behind to implement the edits we had made on a large computer at her desk. As we worked, she paced back and forth across her studio, holding the manuscript before her like a lantern and reading aloud. I captured any mistakes we found, editing on the fly. That particular afternoon, we were polishing a passage on communication: *Saying What You Want and Mean.* It was not such an easy subject to explain, and we ourselves were having trouble knowing what we wanted and saying what we meant. Around three, she came to a halt in the center of the room and announced she was going out for air. I can't see straight, she said. She tucked her crimson hair beneath a scarf and slipped into her coat. Then she was out the door, her footsteps disappearing down the hall.

The last couple sentences she'd read aloud echoed in my brain: *Communication, communication, communication! (There's no shame in lubrication!)* I was feeling suspicious of exclamation marks these days. I nixed one in a dash of red. It was sobering: *There's no shame in lubrication.* I read on: *Lack of desire is the most common complaint* . . . Then I glanced at the clock. The self-help author's breaks could last anywhere from ten minutes to an hour. I took the cordless from its cradle on the desk and held it to my ear.

I dialed my old office from memory, prepared for further disappointment. The women I had known would have families, senior positions at the Met, and who knew what else, I could only remember so many items from their ten-year plans. In any case, they'd gone. As the phone rang, I recalled our lunchtime powwows with some regret, wishing I'd turned out more like them.

Then a woman answered. Hello? It was Constance's assistant. Constance and her supernatural memory! Of course she had her own assistant now. We're old friends, I told the woman on the other end, who connected me directly.

Percy?

I can't tell you how glad I am to hear your voice, I said.

Constance had been promoted. Well, well. Look at you. On the up-and-up. Oh, stop, she said. She filled me in. Who'd gone, who'd stayed. Ten years was a long time—I didn't recognize any of these names. From her office, she could see the famous Rockefeller tree and the tourists twirling on ice. They're wiping out left and right, she reported. That's Constance for you: looking down on the world from on high. I imagined her there. In a corner of glass. Then her keyboard clacked on the line, drawing me back to the favor I'd called to ask. By the way, I said. Have you heard of that gallery, the photographs on view? Of course she had. She even was thinking of acquiring one herself. I paused. Really? Why not? she said. They were wonderful, no? I asked her what she thought of the woman featured in them, lying languid on the bed. She was confused.

I hadn't thought. Why do you ask?

I told Constance the real question we should be asking was why that woman was me. I gave her the facts. The artist was my former fiancé, and I was the woman on the bed. That's my room, I said. My bed. There was a silence on the line. Then the soft tapping of further keys. I wondered if she was taking notes. I could see Constance at her desk, phone pressed to her ear, framed posters from recent auctions reflecting the tourists sliding across the ice. So that's him, then, she finally said. She promised to place some calls on my behalf. I thanked her. I couldn't thank her enough, in fact.

Only, don't call back here! Call me at home.

I finished reciting my number just as the self-help author stepped through the door.

I felt lighter knowing Constance was on my side. Upstairs, I reached into the teapot for more saltines. Misha and I split a deli sandwich. I made too much cucumber salad; it was soothing to chop. Whole bushels reduced to cubes as we talked through those aspects of his presentation that were still weighing on his mind. I hate the finances, he said. I patted his arm. A complaint made only by those who have enough money to start, I replied. He looked at me. That's exactly the problem, he said. We don't. The holiday lights hollowed his cheeks, and the telegraphic notes we'd written to each other made pastel patterns on the wall: *Poetry Reading, Sunday @ 6* and also *Cancel poems!* The kitchenette was narrow and dark, like a confessional, and I felt, for a moment, like divulging. But too often those things that seemed to me worthy of shock and surprise were not so notable to Misha. I could already imagine his answer, the casual shrug, were I to tell him of the exhibition. Sometimes bowls just fall from shelves. Sometimes you mistake yourself for someone else. And some things, I thought, you simply cannot set aside. Misha bit into his sandwich. He lifted an *Am J Tra La* from the stolen scholarship strewn across the table.

What is going on?

Self-help, I replied.

15

At the end of a long Saturday reviewing proofs, the self-help author often stood me in the hall just outside her apartment to sprinkle invisible substances over my head, like a baker powdering a cake. These charms were meant to protect me from the evil corporate forces that governed the streets beyond our doors.

I'm only going to the Village. I'll be fine.

She shook her head.

Doesn't matter where you go, they're everywhere these days.

We'd spent the previous few hours re-articulating what we meant by *Saying What You Mean* and preparing her apartment for the poetry reading. The chairs were drawn into a circle around the coffee table. Empty bowls awaited fancy nuts. From the doorway, I could see past the soft slope of her shoulder, out the window, to the small park where I used to lie on a bench at night when I forgot my keys. The cacti stood in a row along the sill. Usually I was skeptical of the self-help author's protective spells. Today, however, I felt they couldn't hurt.

Actually, can I have an extra?

She looked at me.

Something on your mind?

Just a feeling, I said.

Her hands whirled through the air again.

I had not yet acquired the promised anthology of Eastern European poems. I went in search. At the very least it would take my mind off waiting for Constance to call. The train inched along its weekend schedule, regurgitated me into the market at Union Square, where greens piled high, each row crushing the one below. I stepped on a radish. It resisted. A slow spill crept along the pavement toward the drain. The shops on Broadway seemed once removed from what I remembered, derivatives of brands I couldn't place. I paused on the sidewalk outside the movie theater and gazed up at the marquee. Misha had told me no one knew what the public wanted to watch these days. There were producers who'd ordered the World Trade Center erased from their films, others who'd asked special effects to digitally resurrect it, casting twain shadows against the sky. I felt strange. Perhaps the self-help author's charms were working all too well.

The bookstore was another block. There really were miles of books. I didn't know where to start. Inside, shoppers pushed and pardoned themselves. I moved through the maze and found two clerks on ladders restocking the uppermost shelves of Western Classics. I cleared my throat. Excuse me, I said. I'm looking for the

Poetry section? The one stared at me. This happened from time to time. People stopped me eagerly on platforms, at corners, circled me like a cheap souvenir. *Are you Ukrainian?* Not that I could recall. I wondered what it was he saw in me, whether I struck him as especially familiar, or odd.

End of the aisle, he said.

I took a detour through Cookbooks, then made my way to poems. The shelf devoted to Central, Central Eastern, and/or Eastern European letters was not large. There were only two feet of books from which to choose, and perhaps this was for the best; everyone was writing on war and death. I found a cluster of Poles, self-segregated around a white sticker on the wood: Polish. *After a war*, Szymborska said, *someone has to tidy up*. I read some letters by Miłosz. He made Marxism sound like a housekeeper's dream: . . . *eliminates certain problems by the same principle that the blowing up of a city eliminates marital quarrels, concerns about the furniture, etc.* I was full of questions. The clerks were still on their ladders, and I called to them.

Does Poland count as Eastern Europe?

The space between them seemed to tense as they descended into debate.

I'd say so.

Would you?

The cultural exchange with the West is asymmetrical—

I looked around and imagined all the books going up in flames.

The clerks' voices faded as I took my place in line. At the register, I selected a packet of candies to eat on the train, and on the platform unwrapped the silver foil. I placed a sugar tablet on my tongue. It tasted like soap. I spat it into my palm. The car rattled uptown as I steadied the book in my lap.

> *how difficult it is to remain just one person,*
> *for our house is open, there are no keys in the doors . . .*

I had rather left my whole life unlocked, I thought.

◈

At home, Misha was lying crosswise on the bed, deeply absorbed in some problem of his own. He wore his tweed jacket—his one jacket—and his face was warped the way faces are when seen upside down. Hi, love, he said. Hi, I said. We kissed. Then I locked the bathroom door, turned on the faucet, and tried not to be sick.

16

At the sink, I splashed my face. I washed away smudges of mascara and the self-help author's charms. Then, in a rare breach of my own rules, I went to the bed and placed my damp cheek on Misha's chest. He looked at me, surprised. There was no thinking, no talking for a while. After, we lay for a long time as the light began to fade.

I stared across the room into the channel of the air shaft, waiting for something to fall. Misha folded his hands behind his head, and I watched his breastbone strain against his breath. I drew the blankets to my chin.

I think I've gained some weight.

Misha nodded.

I like it.

You're not supposed to *say* you notice.

Percy, I live with you. Of course I notice things.

<hr />

At midnight, I stood in the kitchenette with the phone, debating whether to call Constance again. The dial tone emanated from my palm. I returned the receiver to its lilac embrace. Everything was quiet. I listened for the roach, for footsteps overhead, the sound of other people's faucets drawing hot water through the walls. I was positive that I was Persephone Q. Who needed proof? Still, it worried me she hadn't called.

Despair seeks an object: I glanced around in search of candidates. The holiday lights illuminated the gleaming kitchenette, the spotless stove. I was running out of things to clean. A dateless calendar of sticky notes advanced across the wall. At the computer, a chime announced the arrival of an incoming message, and my stomach leapt. But it was only another chain email from Yvette. I loaded the message and skimmed the threat within. I'd have bad luck in love, it read, unless I forwarded the message tenfold, fanning fear at an exponential rate. *Sry*, Yvette had added above the body text. *I'm such an idiot about these things . . .*

I'd been avoiding the hospital of late, now that I was beginning to show. My veins adorned my chest in a maze of alarming blue. I'd been gaining weight, as Misha said, though I subsisted mostly on saltines. I hadn't seen Yvette in weeks, though she was my oldest, my closest friend. We were an unlikely pair. She put her confidence in protocols and moral flowcharts: This is what you do, what you don't. The Hippocratic Oath. *I will abstain from all intentional wrong-doing and harm . . .* After my fiancé and I split, I'd sat in her kitchen, drinking tomato juice, as she set about separating our actions like fallen pieces on a game board, bishops from pawns, red from black. We were both guilty, by her assessment. You didn't deliver life-altering news in a letter, as my fiancé had. You did not show up to someone's apartment unannounced, after you'd already moved out, as I had done. Above all, she said, you didn't break off an engagement with the casualness of going for a walk. I loved her anyway.

hey are you around? there's something i want you to see

Her screen name flashed from idle yellow to active green.

(typing . . .)
brb

———

I watched the chatbox, willing her return. The roach shuffled behind the stove. How many times had Yvette seen me sleeping, changing, padding around the dorm in a towel, putting on my bra? We used to trade clothes, Yvette and I. I marauded her closet whenever I had an interview, she plundered mine when we went to the bar. I remembered her leaning against my dresser while wearing my skirt, a faded floral print, and looking down the length of her marvelous legs. I'd rather not look like myself, just for a night, she said.

The computer chimed.

> tmrw?
>
> yes! it'll only take an hour

My reflection was faint in the window of the kitchenette, cast in the blue light of the screen. Yvette knew me almost as well as I did myself. She'd have to recognize me.

17

I slept for sixteen hours. When I woke up, in a panic, I leapt immediately from the bed, relieved to see that Misha was already gone. On his pillow, a Post-it note: *See you tonight, for poems?* I added a smiley and taped it to the wall. Then I sat at the computer and entered *"eleven weeks" AND "what to expect."* Yvette and I had planned to meet at the gallery in the afternoon, and I had a few hours yet. I read about my veins, my feet, the hampered ability to take a shit. The symptoms went on and on, and yet sudden acts of violence against your husband was not one.

In the air shaft, a string of lights had appeared overnight; it sank through the shadows like a slender flame down a magician's throat. I watched the pale torches tap against the brick. I messaged Yvette: *see you soon.* Then I slipped on a coat. Outside, it was just beginning to snow.

⬙

From Misha, I had learned a cardinal rule of the start-up world, adopted after the dot-com bust: entertain the worst. At Insta-Ad, everything was calculated according to a weighted average, and the most important thing to weigh was the greatest failure that could possibly occur. This meant that with a 10 percent chance of losing a million, 90 of making off with a hundred thousand for oneself, estimated earnings left you ten thousand in the hole. The key to such calculations, of course, was that even an infinitesimal probability of losing everything could tip outcomes toward the negative, making your prospective project a very bad gamble indeed. As I walked to the train, head down and hood raised, avoiding flurries, reflections, the stray passerby's gaze, I performed a little estimate of my own. There was an iota of a chance that the receptionist and the mother-and-daughter pair were in fact correct: the woman in the photographs was not me. This iota-sized coefficient, however, applied to an outsized risk. To pursue the cause in error—to insist that I was Persephone Q, when in fact the woman was someone else—meant veritably misidentifying myself. And to do so in front of Misha, my fiancé, the public jury of the internet, only amplified the estimated loss. The whole world would respond with one of Misha's shrugs. The thing to do, I resolved, was reduce the probability that I was wrong to zero. And this struck me as not so difficult— certainty was so close.

I'd borrowed Misha's jacket. It was too large for me, too blue—my usual trench was pink—but it offered breakfast complimentary and continental: I reached into a pocket and found a slice of toast; in the opposite pouch, an orange. I imagined my fiancé breakfasting in some regal teahouse along the park. He must have heard by now of my continued insistence, and yet he refused to entertain the truth. His email slammed like a storm door in my thoughts: *Luck—I don't usually take pictures of Americans.* This was the problem with communication online. Everyone was so accessible, trackable, and yet, like a pop-up, easily dodged. In a way, email wasn't intrusive enough. The web diverts unwanted women into folders full of spam. A pay phone stood a few blocks from the entrance to the train, and I wedged myself through the accordion doors. I'd used this phone only once before, after Harold disappeared, and it was Yvette I'd called. Now I punched in my fiancé's number— what had once been my number—and slipped in the coins. A pre-recorded operator informed me she could not complete my request. With a wave of anxiety, I wondered if he'd moved, bought himself a house in Berkeley, like Miłosz. Then I dialed again, and the call went through. The ringing rolled into the signal to record. I hung up quickly, suddenly afraid to hear his voice.

It was a bit of a struggle, extricating myself from the booth. I stumbled into the street. A passing mother took one glance at me, then pressed her child against her thigh. I wanted to tell her I had a child, too. They hurried into the snow.

Underground, downtown, past the naked corner now stripped of its paper shrine. I met Yvette in the street. She'd arrived in her mint-blue scrubs and opera coat and not in the mood for art at all. I hoped this wouldn't bias her response.

So, she said. What's this about?

Yvette had a way of upturning my hypotheses, rendering them null. I had told her nothing about the exhibition, and so she had no idea of the treatment she was about to receive. Her visit to the gallery was a sort of blind experiment, as the hospital might say. We walked west. At the gallery steps, I paused. I cupped my hands to the glass and peered through the doors. The same receptionist was there, at the enamel desk, beneath her canopy of orchids, and I had no desire to repeat the scene from a few days before. Abruptly, I pulled away. So here's what we'll do, I said. You go in, I'll stay. Then, when you come out, we'll talk about what you think you've seen. Yvette stared at the door. Her dark hair was loose beneath her cap, and snowflakes settled in her curls. Low violet bruises bloomed beneath her eyes from lack of sleep.

Percy, she said wearily. What did you do now?

Nothing.

She studied me a moment.

Well, you look like shit.

She disappeared inside. I stood on the sidewalk, obscured by snow, counting down from ten over and over, like one of Misha's loops: *do i = 10 to 1; n = i; output; end*. I counted the other visitors who entered. Three. Five. Eleven. I tried to catch their eyes as they came and went. But they were absorbed in the tops of their shoes, in each other, in the hazardous descent of the snow-glazed steps. I ran my loop again. As I waited, some of Yvette's more recent accusations returned to me: *Who gets engaged and married in a single day?* I pushed these thoughts aside. I watched a group of art students, college-age, file through the door. A girl draped to her knees in leather reached into her knapsack and produced a dollar. Here, she said. I looked up, surprised. Oh, that's all right. The bill fluttered between us in the snow. I admired her persistence. I gave in. Thanks, I said.

When Yvette reemerged, I fell in beside her. Together, we set off toward the train. The warehouses passed in silence beneath the thick gray sky. Deflated bicycles claimed signposts, rims flush to the cement.

So, what did you think?

Yvette shoved her hands deeper into the pockets of her coat.

Give me a second, she said.

On the train, we slumped. Yvette uncapped a tube of lip balm, applied it, handed the cartridge to me. I had a habit of accepting on reflex whatever Yvette offered. Sometimes it seemed that's all our friendship was, one long one-way street. I slicked on the gloss. On an advertisement overhead, a salivating pup chased a coupon for pet food, redeemable online. I wondered how it was they tracked the impact of those ads, absent direct clicks: *if purchase then n = 1; else* . . . I turned to my friend.

Did you notice the artist?
    Yes.
    And the woman in the photographs?
    Yvette looked into the woolen palms of her gloves.
    It doesn't *not* look like you, she said.
    I told her how the exhibition book had arrived at my door, unmarked. How I'd opened it late at night to find my furniture, my walls, my view. The red was a red you never forget. I told her it happens sometimes, in life, that you fail to see yourself as you are. And then, all at once, you do.
    That's my room.
    Yvette thumbed a highlight of gloss from her chin.
    Even if it was, what good can come of insisting that everyone know?
    You don't believe me.
    That's not true.
    Then why won't you agree?
    It's just—it seems a little unlikely.

The train careened through a turn. I spoke over the shrill cry of the tracks, and this lent an unpleasant, exclamatory quality to everything I said next. That's the difference between you and Misha, I told her. He respects what I think. I expounded on the foundations of love, and how its cornerstone was exactly what Misha and I had: profound agreement. I told her I didn't care about prudence or good sense or planning ahead. For once, I did not want to follow her moral flowcharts to the end. She ought to simply take me at my word. Yvette studied the pet food ad for many stops. Then she shook her head.

Sometimes, Percy, I think you can't be happy with what you have.

We crawled to a halt at Manhattan's eastern edge. Aboveground, I followed her to the hospital, walking north on York. The shops thinned and the streets cleared. The wind came in off the river cold and sharp. Yvette tried to persuade me to see things from her point of view. She reminded me what I had been like when I was with my fiancé. You weren't yourself around him, she said. You got competitive. Also kind of mean. I nodded. Only I seemed to remember it differently. I didn't recall it being so trying—I had agreed to marry him, after all. But I suppose certain frames go missing from ten years of film. That I could concede. I trailed her through the hospital doors, where teams of doctors and other personnel glided across the linoleum sheen, crowded into elevators. Yvette checked her pager, pocketed it again. She had a few minutes. Do you want something to eat? she said. She stood with her opera coat folded over an arm, plain in her uniform. She was already distant, distracted. Part of me wanted very much to accept, to follow her to the cafeteria and, over a steaming slice of quiche, ask if the exhaustion, the nausea, the swelling I felt all over, as if my body were attempting to molt, if these things were normal after all. I felt like a tired child who's been offered a bed. Yet there was something in accepting, I knew, that would amount to giving up, giving in, a quid pro quo agreement never to mention the exhibition again. I smiled.

No, thanks.

Yvette lingered another moment.

Are you sure?

I nodded. She turned to go.

Wait, I said. If it isn't me, then who? Who is that in the pictures, in *my very room?*

Yvette placed a firm hand on my arm.

I don't think it matters now.

Defeated, I looked around at the sea of interns sleepwalking through their shifts in scrubs. They swept me up in a current of green, deposited me in the ER waiting room. I took a seat. I was inclined to stay here until Yvette's break, when I might reconcile our perspectives. I always found it distressing when she and I did not see the world the same. There was a time, in college, when we, too, had agreed profoundly. We made unanimous decisions about when to study, what to eat, whether wooden sandals could be worn with socks (indeed). Things had changed. I wished she'd lived with me back when I was the sole occupant of my red room, and so borne witness to that crimson era. I drew into the hood of Misha's jacket, depressed. The ER was sparsely populated. There was a TV mounted to the ceiling, and I tuned in to a documentary on British royalty. I watched a princess emerge from a car, signature clutch pressed to her chest, concealing cleavage. My own breasts protested against the zipper of the otherwise enormous coat. Across the room, a woman rocked in a chair nailed to the floor as if for the express purpose of keeping her in place. She reached into her purse, extracted a hot dog wrapped in foil. It had all the fixings: mustard, onions, relish. She ate. She withdrew a second hot dog from the bag. Then another, another. At least four more frankfurters emerged, and, transfixed, I watched her consume them all before I realized it was time to go, Yvette would not be coming back.

18

I went for a long walk. Out the sliding hospital doors, heading west. Ambulances faded. Delis disappeared from corners as the rents began to rise. Doormen guarded awnings, and the avenues grew wide. The side streets distended rarefied stoops and delivered me, finally, to museum row, where kiosks claimed the curbs, pumping halal steam.

It was a long time since I'd been to the Met. I no longer knew where anything was. I used to visit on some of my more ambitious wanderings at night, back when Harold still lived across the hall. I liked to sit on the steps, long after the galleries had closed, and watch the mansions across the avenue for flashes of life. It was never long before a policeman came to shoo me away. Now I passed through the double doors and into the lobby, where I lowered the hood of Misha's coat. Flower arrangements erupted from the keystone of a vase. A mother dragged her daughter, a little flower herself festooned in fuchsia hat and bow, down the hall to see sarcophagi. The museum was filled with children at this hour, and I tried to imagine the apartments from whence they came: juice boxes in the cupboards, small stools to reach the sink. At the ticket booth, I paid what I wished. Then I went in search of period rooms. I used to love those preserved interiors, whole rooms imported from afar. I went whenever I had the urge to visit someone else's home. In the American Wing, I found Europe instead: a bedroom exhumed from the ashes of Pompeii. It had been dusted, deconstructed, airlifted, to appear among the galleries frescoed in red and trompe l'oeil. I longed to crawl into a Venetian four-poster in the following display, replete with matching bedroom set, and close my eyes. The wallpaper was reminiscent, I imagined, of the silver algae in the Grand Canal. Tourists lifted cameras into sight lines. *So that's what it was like.* The object labels agreed: . . . *curators used to aim to create a "period feeling," such as in the Nur al-Din room, in order to capture an* emotional *or* atmospheric *truth. More recently, however, the standard has been to re-create each room in exact detail* . . . In the Syrian reception hall, a fountain gurgled over tiles of olive, amber, toothy white, and velvet ropes barred entry. Because that's the thing, with fantasy. You have to stay on your side. I passed through a roomful of clocks competing for the hour in syncopated chimes, made my way outside.

At the edge of the park, I looked back into the glass greenhouse of the Egyptian Wing, where I caught a glimpse of the fussy bow. The little girl was splashing fuchsia in the reflecting pool. I turned up the path. The obelisk rose gray in the garden, blocking sun. How far it was from home.

◆

Back at the apartment, I heard from Constance again. The phone rang, and I lunged for it. The news was not good. Honey, she said. Are you sure there hasn't been some mistake? I was sure. I insisted on the familiarity of the scene. The bed. The view. I had lived there a whole year, I said, before moving in with my fiancé. She sighed. As far as I can tell, no one knows who the woman in the pictures is. Not even the artist himself. There was a long and awkward pause.

Sweetheart, she said. Don't you have any evidence at all?

19

It was unsettling to think that so many of the people who mattered in my life didn't believe me when I told them who I was. That is me, I said. It's me in the photographs. No one seemed to value my conviction. Yvette and Constance were the most perceptive women I knew. I admired them both for being so incisive and opinionated where I was not. I knew they wouldn't lie, not even by omission. And yet, while I would have readily deferred to them in nearly every other matter, I was sure that in this one instance they were wrong. I was reminded that the people closest to you suffer from a bias. They get used to your habits, used to your face. They hardly see you at all.

That evening, Misha and I attended the poetry reading. I put some effort into my hair. The self-help author greeted us at the door, her own locks offset by a bright green blouse. Thank you, love, she said, when I handed her the book. It has Miłosz, I pointed out. Her heels, leopard-print, clacked across the exceptionally clean floors as she ferried it to the shelves. The poets milled about the coffee table, snacking on cubes of cheese. We joined. These readings were organized rather like the clubs of which the ex–professional dancer spoke, by word of mouth, and so the crowd was always shifting. Only the self-help author knew everyone by name. She opened another bag of crackers and poured the rounds into a bowl. Misha, she said, put that wine here. Doyle, I saved your seat. Katherine, she said to a woman with a foam brace belted darkly around her middle, how is the back? Buck was a regular not even I could forget. He'd suffered a flash of frostbite the year before, and the sore was slowly tracking its way across the pale bridge of his nose. Buck, the self-help author said when he arrived, you have *got* to get that checked. He hesitated in the doorway, leaning on his cane, then shuffled unevenly across the room, making a beeline for the Brie.

The poets had been in New York all this time. They grumbled about how the city had changed, how they missed the metropolis of decades past. They mourned the sixties, the eighties, the bars that had closed. The sailors, they said, had disappeared. As had the docks. They'd seen everything, these poets, and perhaps this was what made them so ruthless when it came to judging verse. There was a high bar for audience applause, and if a poem was no good, it was met with silence. I don't think you could have paid me, really, to read a poem of my own. I touched my hair. I missed saltines. Misha and I were among the very few not actively practicing lines, and I watched the nervous woman at my side mumble stanzas to herself. She paused now and then to slip a note card from her breast pocket. Her eyes darted across the text. Boots of lead, she said softly. *Boots of lead. Boots of lead.* The poem returned to the folds of her floral shirt as she continued reciting under her breath, lips moving soundlessly over the rhymes.

I must have been staring. A cracker broke in my hand when I missed my mouth and hit my chin. I went searching for the crumbs. I wore a mauve velvet dress that billowed over my belly, though the bust was tighter than it had ever been. When I glanced down, my own breasts seemed to me obscene. Misha whispered as I fished in my bra.

What are you doing?

Stand in front of me.

When I glanced up again, cracker retrieved, Doyle was sitting in his usual chair in front of the buffet, looking noticeably subdued. Normally he sang under his breath. He wore pastels. Often he had the final say. Today, however, his suit was deliberately drab, and when he spoke he was pensive, fingers tented beneath his jaw. He was saying something about the trains, the long tunnels at Times Square that he took to work. I feel so *unsafe*, he said. Katherine and the other readers resounded agreement, replaced celery sticks on paper plates. Misha cavalierly crunched a carrot.

I wouldn't worry, he said.

I was familiar with Misha's opinions regarding American fear. In the weeks after the towers fell, when we were mostly lying in my bed, trading discs and Discmans, he had expressed confusion. The national response streamed into our room through every available outlet: the radio, the telephone, the muffled murmur of the pundits on the television next door. Even Misha's friends at home, in Sofia, were consuming American footage, American news. The radio reported the national traffic, the bumper-to-bumper queues that snaked through the plains like kudzu as SUVs lined up outside of gas stations, for gas. I wondered what I'd missed. Where was everyone driving, that they found it so crucial to refill the tank? Misha, flat on his back in my bed, slipped his headphones from his ears. To Americans, he said, war is always elsewhere. Maybe they were driving there. He stretched his arms over his head, as he did whenever he was lost in thought. The sun was bright in the sheets. I didn't know if he was right or not. I found it difficult to generalize about my country. That was the trouble—I deferred. The radio purred. I listened to the absence of the rumbling of trains. Maybe it was true, as Misha said, that war took place abroad, but at the moment it felt near. Or nearer. Or at least, in the rest of the city, the subject was still raw. Lower Manhattan was raw, a whole block ragged and agape, and the self-help author's apartment was crowded with poets who were still struggling to assign verse to the rupture of that day. It wasn't exactly the place, I thought, for Misha to expound on his personal views. I reached for his shoulder to tell him to leave things be—were we not here for poems?—but he was already too far along. You live in one of the safest places on earth, he was saying, in one of the most powerful empires ever known. He waved a spear of cheese cubes like a tiny plastic sword.

This is one of the safest cities around.

Doyle raised his eyebrows.

Have you ever walked these streets as a black man?

Obviously not, Misha said.

I was downtown that day, said someone else.

So was I.

Another poet wondered, in a whisper, *Where is this guy from?*

Misha flourished his cheese kebab.

Statistically speaking, the trains are very safe. So I am only saying there's no need to feel afraid of additional terrorism on subways—

The woman who'd wondered as to Misha's origins sat back in her seat. Katherine crossed her arms over the straps of her body brace, as if daring Misha to go on. I looked to the corner, where the self-help author was still pleading with Buck, exhorting him to find help for his sore. I placed a hand on Misha's arm.

Misha, I said quietly. Maybe not right now.

The self-help author tapped a spoon against a glass, sent around a bottle of wine. Then the poems commenced. A tensile silence set-tled over the cheese as, one by one, each poet stood to read. This is a poem about a mermaid, a man began. And by mermaid I mean a woman I once loved. The woman with the floral blouse and note cards in her pockets, thoughts of leaden boots, lulled the room into an iambic dream. A Plank in Treason broke / And I Fell down, and down. That's plagiarism, Doyle said. But it was a nice poem, in the end. There were nature poems and odes. A man with multiple totes hanging from either shoulder stood and read from the wrinkled receipt in his hand: Listen to the waters laughing / Feel the moonlight hug you / Look up into a diamond sky and countless miles of blackness / Listen, feel, look and watch / Taste the sweet summer air / These are the things of the night / To which nothing can compare.

Misha's applause was the only sound in the room. I like it, it's simple, he said. Too simplistic, Doyle replied. Who would ever disagree with a poem like that? The self-help author interrupted. Since when was polemic the purpose of an ode? I glanced at the atlases on the walls. The whole world was at our shoulder blades. Across the room, Buck slouched in a stool, one leg crossed elegantly over the other, nose bent toward the anthology I'd brought. Each time he turned a page he closed his eyes and paused. I stared at the deep sore in the center of his face. It poured slowly over his features, like a lava spill, abutting the smooth skin of his cheeks. The wound had a gravity that drew me in. The room, the food, the atlases and snacks, the sound of other people's voices, fell away. Buck must have sensed me staring. He opened his eyes, looked up from his poems. His gaze met mine. I had the feeling then that I had gotten it wrong. I had no such gravity, I thought, at the center of myself.

20

A whole week had passed without my making any headway against the exhibition. Ditto my fiancé's email. The only real progress was with respect to keeping house—I'd developed a passion for keeping the apartment alarmingly pristine. The stove shone like a commercial. The floorboards were bright with wax. The whole apartment reeked of ammonia. No more cleaning, Misha said. Instead I cooked. I chopped and broiled and trimmed. After the poetry reading, I set to work on the ultimate audition of a cook's ability to concassé: the ratatouille. Bowls crowded the credenza. I used all the bowls we had, in fact. The doors to the cupboards swung wide, the shelves within bereft, as if we'd been burgled. I rescued those onions from the refrigerator and finally reduced them into a sordid soup. It was tranquilizing, watching the translucent rings brown to a deep caramel. I found it pleasant to be with Misha. He was my only comfort at the time, the only person around whom I felt compos mentis—even if I was, to him, a threat. And this made it all the more important not to tell my husband about the other me, the one who posed on gallery walls. I didn't want to lose him, too.

I stood at the credenza, thoughts still attuned to iambic verse, slicing plum tomatoes. Misha was on the bed, going over his accounts. He was sullen after the scene downstairs.

Misha.

Yes?

I started to say one thing, then changed course.

Would you say Bulgaria is Balkan or European? And if European, Central or Eastern?

He chewed his pen.

It's complicated. Depends on who you ask.

I brought him a tomato steak doused with salt, sat on the edge of the bed. I felt tenderly toward my husband. I missed evenings like this. The two of us at home, working on our separate tasks. I lay back on the mattress, watched his ribs press against the cotton of his shirt as he swallowed. He jotted something on his palm.

They have a point downstairs. But still, it is no reason to go to war.

I don't think anyone meant that, I said.

What about all the ones who do?

At least we're not related to them.

He nodded.

I wonder if I'd feel differently if I had kids.

I rose in a cool shock of alarm.

What do you mean?

Misha shrugged, reached for my thigh.

I mean, who knows what is going through your mind once you are having a child?

He ran a hand through my hair, kissed me, drew his feet onto the bed. Cross-legged, he returned to his accounts. I folded my hands over the velvet bodice of my dress, suddenly distraught. It bothered me that, of the two of us, Misha seemed the one more naturally disposed to motherhood.

At three in the morning, zucchini peels slid slick as fish across the floor, Misha was in bed, and I was at the sink, wrapping a bandage around my thumb. One moment I had been whole and dexterous, and in the next a pink chasm burrowed, like a geological event, through the flat of my nail bed. I looked helplessly at the red isthmus to which the corner of my nail clung. I had half a mind to finish the job. Instead I wrapped it in a bandage, eliciting pain. Then I turned on the faucet and vomited into the sink.

On those rare evenings when I am feeling truly low, when not even the library, Encarta, Napster, beauty blogs, the self-help author's website and message box, asking Jeeves or the AIM chatbot, when not even the porn star or the scientist can effect some improvement in my mood, I take refuge on the roof. The roof will remind you that in the grander scheme of things, you are doing okay. So Misha always said. Our building was seven stories tall and it was true that from this vantage the world was much improved. Outside, I breathed in the cool syrup of the night and felt my nausea calm. I nursed my thumb. The laundry I had hung the day before floated on the line, laced with snow. Misha's sleeves tangled with mine. Bras lifted and fell like sighs. I caught one. The cups were half frozen and stiff.

I released a sweater from its clothespins and pulled it over my head. It was my mother's, though I had been wearing it since I was young.

Down below, Manhattan unfurled itself into 4:00 a.m. Traffic flowed through the avenues, soft and steady as waves. Misha had installed a lawn chair by the balustrade in the summer, and I reached between the plastic belts of the seat for the biscuit tin in which I kept a stash of cigarettes. Inside, a book of matches and three packs of Camel Lights. I had smoked sporadically for many years—what else is there to do, on late-night walks?—but after Misha moved in, my cigarettes had begun to disappear. I'd counter-hid them in this tin. I looked into the shallow basin now, lit a Camel, then immediately tossed it into the street. Leaning over the balustrade, I watched it flutter to the ground. I reached for another. *Luxury Assorted*, advised the biscuit lid.

I was still at the cornice, trying not to smoke, when I heard someone at the hatch. The door swung slightly open. It was barely ajar. Then a woman slunk through the narrow gap. It was Claire from across the hall. Her eyes were swollen and sad and settled on me with a kind of quiet greed, as if finding me here, on the roof, might sate some kind of hunger. Her running tights shimmered with patterns, and over these she wore a loose cranberry sweater. I tucked my thumb, concealing gauze. She delicately cleared her throat.

Could I have one of those?

I offered her the tin.

Have them all, I said. I'm trying to quit.

21

I can't say I'd ever really taken to Claire. She was the sort of woman whose athletic apparel matched. Who knows why I accepted the invitation, then, to join her in her apartment that night. I suppose I was lonely. Her nails flared pinkly on the banister as I followed her down the stairs and into her unit, where she cracked the window and groped through drawers. She lifted the top of Harold's old desk, searching for an ashtray.

It's in here somewhere, she said.

Whenever I saw Claire, it seemed she was always going for or returning from a jog. She took off daily and at length through the sloping paths of Central Park. She went early and much too late. I heard her in the hours I couldn't sleep—I could always tell it was her footsteps on the stairs, because she took them two at a time, bounding. Had I ever enjoyed such a salubrious state, perhaps I, too, would have developed an appreciation for exertion. But as I had not, it seemed to me a public nuisance and its benefits opaque. The self-help author was especially bewildered by this prodigal display of energy. Poor Claire, she said. There were other people who endured whole lifetimes of suffering and managed not to go insane.

The last time I'd found myself inside 4C was soon after Harold disappeared. I remembered opening the door to look in on Claire, casserole in hand, and being struck dumb with surprise: every surface teetered with exquisite bijouterie. A transparent elephant, a Tiffany lamp. The shelves and end tables crowded with pitchers and the ripe gleam of blown-glass fruits. I was very careful making my way into the kitchen, so as not to set off a shrill and icy hum. The whole apartment, really, tinkled faintly when you walked. Meanwhile, the cat leapt among the menagerie of baubles and lemonade pitchers, nudged paperweights. I stood very still, afraid to lift an elbow. I was almost relieved when Claire locked the door against the world and banished us to the hall.

It was in this fragile state that 4C had remained. The glass glowed dimly. I watched Claire's brittle hands as she lit a cigarette, pulled strings on lamps. There was something glassy, I felt, about Claire herself. It struck me she was much better suited to looking after this apartment whenever Harold went away. As he had. Quite permanently, in fact.

I looked around for some record of disruption. The figurines were all in place. The glass elephant raised its miniature trunk over the mantel. There were no women's coats by the door, no ladies' magazines. Aside from the collection of fragile curios, the only other clue of Claire's arrival that I could find was a single pair of running sneakers on the mat by the door.

You sure you don't want one?

I shook my head.

Claire studied the pack in her hands.

I quit, too, she said, but I suppose I've been on edge.

She looked so dejected, snapping the lighter in front of her face, that I found myself blurting out, I would join you, really, it's just I'm pregnant. She considered me, Camel poised.

Congratulations, she said.

She smoked. I drank my tea. I told her again how much I'd always admired Harold and his work, that I regretted our having grown apart. Perhaps because I had expressed concern, or simply because she felt compelled to fill the silence, Claire began to relate to me the story of how she and Harold met.

She said:

There is a time in every woman's life when you can have whatever you want. I was that age. My senior year, I lived in a dorm right there on Broadway. That summer I won an internship at the publishing house. It was a big deal. I bought myself a skirt. I felt really on top of the world. It must have had an effect. People noticed me that summer. They remembered me. The man at the coffee cart said, Hey, beautiful. Every morning. Hey, beautiful, he said. At the office people came by my desk. Harold was one of them. Except he was different. He was older, for one, and didn't talk much. He'd make these little observations about the weather, the city, the illustrations he was working on. He wasn't in every day, but I was running into him whenever he was. I saw him at the water cooler. At lunch. He waited for me at the elevators to walk me to the train. I could have reported him, but I guess I found it sweet. I told him he was too old for me. He didn't seem to mind. He never really cared about that kind of thing. Then the summer was over, and I left. He sent me letters. They were forwarded all the way to California, and in them he asked me how was school. I reminded him I'd graduated. That I'd moved home, probably for good. I really thought that'd be it for Harold and me. For a while I didn't think about him at all. Probably I would have forgotten him completely. Then the emails started. I wonder how he found my address. He wanted to know how I was, how he could help. I told him there wasn't much I needed help with, and so he wrote about other things. Small things. Something he saw out his window. Out this window, I guess. He'd tell me what he ate for lunch. He sent poems. I really started to look forward to those emails, you know? It ruined my day, if he didn't write. But you know how it is online. How easy it is to fall in love with someone who's far away. I told myself it wouldn't be the same in person, if he ever came to visit. Then he did, and it was. He said all the usual little things. Look at those bougainvilleas in the street. That mural on a wall. Lighten up, he said. He came a few times, always for work. Only, what cartoonist travels? This went on for years. Until one day he asked me to come back with him. I said yes. Then it was the two of us, here. He used to talk through his ideas with me. I gave him suggestions for his comics. It's stupid, but I like to think I was a little bit Vera to his Vlad. Or whatever. I still have those emails. I read them all the time.

Winter sifted through the open window, and we watched the curtains breathe. Seated in the armchair, in a beam of streetlight, Claire reminded me of a Penelope, or a Helen, perched at a window with an Adriatic view; outside, the city flashed the plankton of its restless streets. I picked at the bandage on my thumb. The white gauze was now stained a deep maroon.

You must miss him.

Claire shrugged.

He'll be back.

I sipped cold tea. The trees reflected in the windows of the building across the avenue, foliage fragmented in the darkened panes. I felt I'd been unfair to Claire. I felt many things, chief among them loss. Outside, notices cropped up in bursts, like desperate plants, clambering over telephone poles, the entrances to trains, fences, the gallery. The city was filled with pictures of people who'd gone to work one day and never come home, and it seemed almost plausible that Harold had been one of them. Still, the police brushed Claire aside. They were completely overwhelmed. There was no time to spare on a woman mad with heartbreak. Meanwhile, she ran.

She became absorbed in her sweater, smoothing the wool before her like a newspaper she was trying to read. I watched her lift away a tuft of fur. For months, I had only ever seen Claire in the violet windbreaker. That evening, however, she wore the dressy geometric tights and the cranberry sweater to which the cat's fur clung. She'd applied makeup. She was beautiful, I thought. I noticed a hint of blush on her cheeks. Shadow softened her eyes. For whom? She looked lovely there in the pale light from the street. Lovely and severe. I tried to remember if she had always drawn attention this way, if she'd been beautiful all along, but I could not. I looked out the window. I nursed my tea.

You know, I said, something strange happened to me the other day.

Claire looked up from her ministrations to the wool.

Oh?

For at least the third time since I had left the gallery, I told the story of *The Exhibition of Persephone Q*. My search. The surprise I felt. The receptionist's disbelief. In the warmth of Claire's attention, I became more loquacious than I had been in days.

I said:

To be honest, I never really thought my fiancé would make it in the arts. We knew so many people who wanted to back then. Success was not a trend. Though I suppose he was a little more resilient than the rest. He snapped the shutter every few blocks, searching for tableaus. Sometimes I felt I was collected on such a search. I was also a tableau. He used to joke about making art of me. At the time it seemed benign. The idea flattered me, I guess. He was always telling me things about myself that I had missed. No one lives as literally, Percy, as you try to live. It isn't practical at all. He had endless opinions about who I was and what I ought to do. I was too smart, too stupid, too smart in a way that made me stupid, I should write a book. In bed, he traced the moles on my back. You must be Slavic, he said, with moles like that. I felt clearer around him, the way a little anger always focuses your head. I wrote a poem. I wore my hair pinned up in Swedish braids. I kept a diary of everything

I thought. Then, one day, I remembered that it had been a performance all along. Or maybe he reminded me. It was all so long ago. In any case, I left. I never heard from him again. Then, last week, this package arrived. And what do I find inside but a catalog of his show? He's become some kind of sensation. And he's done it by way of using me after all. Which is to say I'm the subject of his exhibition. The only trouble is, it's hard to see who I am. That's the funny thing. No one believes me. Not even my best friends. They think I'm picking at old wounds, making false connections. Not even the internet is on my side. Every search comes up blank. And the worst part is, I don't have any proof. I never was one for photographs or keepsakes. I threw a lot of things away. Whole storage lockers, really. Now I can't help but think. All that evidence! But how was I to know beforehand what was worth keeping, what was trash?

Claire slumped against the wings of the chair, listening. As I spoke, I kept having to shift my eyes away from her, out the window or into my tea, and whenever I returned my gaze I found that hers had never moved. I pressed at the bandage on my thumb. I looked at her, then away.

I have an idea, she said.

She disappeared into the other room. I could hear drawers being opened, papers riffled through. A binder chirped as the rings were pried apart. She returned with an index card in hand. On it was printed the telephone number and email address of a journalist at the *Times*. Claire spoke rapidly and with conviction. This journalist was a friend of hers, well aware of her predicament. She wanted to help, she'd said. She really did. Run a story. Raise awareness. Whatever she could do. Except she was on the culture desk, and a single disappearance wasn't news.

But two disappearances, and one of them art? Now, that's an event, Claire said.

I'd like to say I was aware of the severe contrast between our situations. That I realized my own elision was not at all the same. That it was rather the opposite problem, in fact, to have been made too visible for comfort. But I'm afraid, in the moment, I was rather focused on myself. When Claire told me what a story we would make together, she and Harold and I, I readily agreed. I was seduced. I found myself consenting eagerly to everything she said. I may even have egged her on. I nodded when she insisted that a journalist need not even take us at our word. Publicity was the aim. I would have agreed to anything, I was so relieved to have met someone who shared my view: I was Persephone Q.

Before I knew it, I had acquiesced to a meeting with the journalist and Claire. We'd tell all, and at once. Tomorrow, Claire said. I'll knock. She reminded me that I was not to give up. The air was tense with the shiver of glass, and I felt so full of gratitude I could hardly speak. At the door, I turned to thank her. Then I paused. In the light of the hall, Claire's face seemed strange. I studied her, confused. I saw she had applied makeup to only one of her wide and lustrous eyes. Her whole face seemed off-balance, Picassoesque, and the tilt only worsened when she smiled.

Two women whom no one will believe? You have to admit, it's the perfect weekend read.

I slept for a few hours at the credenza, dreaming of that eye.

22

I still had not responded to my fiancé's email. I woke up in the kitchenette, nauseated and ravenous, with a digit that more resembled a date than an opposable thumb. I mangled the mouse. On the computer, I sifted through the folder where I'd saved my many drafts.

> 12/10 2:01 AM
> What do you mean you don't take pictures of Americans? I looked you up—multiple times. Aside from me, all you've shown is self-portraits!

> 12/12 12:14 PM
> There must be better ways to get even with an ex. What else do you think the internet is for??

> 12/13 7:38 PM
> I'm not threatening, I just don't understand why you won't admit it's me.

> By the way—I'm MARRIED.

None of these seemed right.

I navigated to AOL to check in on the women of the waxing kits.

pandaBRR: Lol
Anjul45: poor kid! ask ur mom.

I scrolled and scrolled and, to my surprise, failed to reach the bottom of the page. It was becoming a popular thread:

Roequentin609: wat matters is that its ur CHOICE. like ur DYING for
    smooth cooch bc that's just who u are at <3. only a problem if ur
    pleasing ur wo/man or whatever out of some DUTY. u read? so wrt
    to original q, i say u wax only as often as u feel is right for u!!
Panopticus: umm sry but prescription of 'u do u!' presupposes freedom
    of thought > freedom of choice >> total myth bc we all grew up in
    sick racist misogynist society internalizing the shit they flush down
    airwaves to keep white male patriarchy alive.
Nicomachean: Hello. I am glad to have stumbled upon such a lively
    debate. It is my belief that manipulation of free will is an oft-
    overlooked component in contemporary discussions of structural
    violence. Roequentin and Panopticus offer excellent summaries of
    modernist and structuralist approaches here. It is easy to forget,
    however, that the concept of free will is itself predated by the idea
    of chance, for which concept we are indebted to the classical world.
    Accident and serendipity productively rupture the predetermined
    course of cosmic fate. Within such fissures, one is able to ask: What
    if? What next? And is not free will predicated on such opportunities
    for imagination? In which case, one ought to welcome into one's life

some element of chance, including as a component of one's choice to wax. As a leading scholar of classical and early modern thought, I invite you to read more about this in my book, *Heraclitus to Aristotle: Why the Ancient World Matters for Americans Today*, forthcoming from Nebraska University Press. Also check out my website: http://www.classix.org. Also I will be signing books after my talk at NYPL on March 12, 2002, at 7:30 p.m. I have a Ph.D.

AnonymousScotsman: It has been shown in exhaustive and largely overlooked treatises on human nature (overlooked at least by those for whom reading has become a form of amusement that precludes serious study) . . . it has been shown, by those still capable of earnest inquiry, that the mind grasps nothing but that which it holds in perceptions. In other words, behind each simple idea is a simple impression, gained through experience. The complex idea is constituted, more complexly, of linked impressions, which as a network may or may not resemble the simple impressions from which it has been derived. For example, consider a world in which people renounce the ego and agree henceforth to act rationally, with dignity, without delusion and against all hope, a world I may happily and readily consider despite the fact that such a world is something I myself have not as yet EXPERIENCED in aggregate. The constituent parts of dignified, humble, and rational behaviors, however—and however rare—are phenomena I have encountered in the observable world and upon which I have reflected. They become fantastical only in connection and extrapolation, such that the complex idea formed by their amalgamation NO LONGER RESEMBLES the observable world. And yet the combination is imaginable nonetheless. Since all impressions depend on experience and as such are proved to be furnished by means other than a priori knowledge, it follows that most ideas are as dubious as we are. Which is to say, as dubious as human experience. Only those conclusions that do NOT depend on existential and/or experiential impressions can be known certainly in any superlative sense of the word. For example, the simple sum of 2 + 2 may be shown to yield 4, indefinitely. But even this is in fact no a priori axiom but an inference dependent on the experience of 2s. It is possible, of course, that some other philosopher in this estimable comment section has gathered such an existential familiarity with the 2 as to eliminate all doubt of its a priori truth, but speaking solely for myself, this is a numerical sense-impression I have never nor indeed ever hope to strip of the mystery of experience. And yet I am quite able to buy groceries, follow recipes, and compute change all the same. I need no certainty of 2 in order to wield the idea of the 2. In all other matters, likewise, we face the inconvenient truth of doubt. It would appear that most of the subjects about which we care to make claims, including identity and causation and whether or not to wax, are relegated to the category of probable as opposed to certain knowledge. We may CONJECTURE that apparently causal relationships such as that observed between fire and smoke may IN THE FUTURE HOLD. However, these inferences are predicated on the assumption that the future will be like the past—THE SUN WILL RISE TOMORROW—rather than on certain knowledge that fire causes smoke. But pity she who does not also assume that one day the future may change! And rudely! Thus, the prudent thinker refrains from the temptation of making bolder claims to certainty. She is left to reckon with the unknowability of the self. For while I must grant to my estimable colleagues here the POSSIBILITY of having observed themselves—THEIR VERY SELVES—I, like most, lack the proper distance for the empirical study of who and what I am. In contemplating my SELF I find nothing more than a collection of perceptions. This is not to conclude that the SELF does not exist at all, but only that we cannot know whether it does or not. It is a mystery. As are the laws that govern its behavior and according to which it is subject to moral judgment. Certainly morality, the oughts and ought-nots, are not nearly so self-evident as arithmetic. Would that universal laws dropped like forbidden fruit from some forbidden tree! (And whether such a tree of knowledge—which, by the way, was theorized to produce pomegranates, not conceptions—ever existed is of course impossible to know, for reasons that to even the half-conscious reader will now seem obvious.) Panopticus is quite right to cast suspicion on the above claims to authenticity, though she does so for the wrong reasons entirely. Truth claims to authenticity are judgments made not by REASON but by EXPERIENCE. By which a priori law can one judge an action as authentic? None! WHICH ACTIONS ARE EVEN SUBJECT TO MORAL JUDGMENT? Excuse my emphasis. But even if such an a priori order were to exist (and it doesn't), one could counter that reason never motivated the sentient being, who is influenced instead by passion and feeling. Lacking a priori criteria, the individual judges the morality of her actions but ex post facto, according to her impression of the impression the act has made on those around her. Thus she EXPERIENCES the moral effect as a collection of SENSE-IMPRESSIONS. On these impressions she bases her ideas of morality and authenticity, according to which she may judge the action she has performed. In other words, U DO U insofar as the DO is something that U expect, given past experience—because one assumes here that the future will be like the past—that others would perceive to be moral and good. To wax or not to wax is a question whose answer can be framed only as a claim of PROBABLE as opposed to CERTAIN knowledge based on your past EXPERIENCE of others' perceptions of your actions. As for Ph.D.s, I'd rather tutor lunatics. Humbly yours, yuppie1967: fuck all ya'll. waxing's only a thing because of porn.

I was strangely moved: yuppie1967, in that moment, felt like the only friend I had.

Claire and my cause had seemed so valiant to me the night before, in front of an audience of glass. Outside the theater of that evening, however, it appeared a misguided scheme. I thought of what the receptionist at the gallery had said: I was free to go to the press. It was my right. But it occurred to me now, in the morning gray of the kitchenette, that in exercising it I would be playing straight into her hands. The press was on the gallery's side. As for approaching the artist, my fiancé—this was also my right. Who could deny it? The cursor hovered for a long moment over the dialog box before I typed a lackluster reply.

qwerty123: thx <3

My wound had burrowed deeper in the night, sinking a sunset through my thumb. I changed my bandage at the sink. I had half a mind to go return the knives, demand a refund—they'd rather assaulted me, after all, and I ought to be compensated for that. I had hoped they might transform me into a cook, maybe a mother. How utterly they had failed me. I gathered the blades into their sheaths. The receipt was still taped to the wall.

Something about these beauty posts told me it was not wise to yoke my fate to Claire's. I was on my own. The idea of the storage locker had begun to haunt me. I wished once again that I hadn't been so hasty clearing it. Perhaps I'd even thrown away a copy of Persephone Q herself. Oh, but could I have used those photographs now! I longed for them so thoroughly, in fact, that for a moment I convinced myself they must be near. It was my apartment against me, at war for the evidence that I was sure it hid.

Misha had already left for the Rockaways. For the Rockaways, then his presentation. I bolted the door. Then I divided the apartment into five—the kitchenette, the bed, the bath, the closet, and the shelves—just as my mother used to do when I was growing up. When I was a child, I lost crucial school-related missives so often that she devised a special system: sectioning the house, she'd comb each territory separately and in order of likelihood. A similar approach had once been used by the U.S. Navy, she explained, to retrieve a nuclear warhead that had slipped, accidentally, from a bomber into the Mediterranean Sea, during what was technically a time of peace. As a method of retrieval, it was endlessly scalable.

I regarded the chaos of my single room. At least it wasn't a sea.

I began with the bed, which seemed most charged with mystery, and so most likely to be withholding information. I stripped the duvet, the pillowcases. I lifted a corner of the mattress and looked beneath. There, spread across the springs, was a dress I had not worn in many years. I must have placed it there in order to press the pleats, the way I'd read about in Russian novels. I slipped it on over my jeans, examined my reflection in the mirror. The wool skirt swished. When I slipped my hand into the pockets, my fingers met a dog-eared photograph. I held it to the light. It was a wallet-sized portrait. Of my fiancé. The purview cleaved to his face, centered his large, bored eyes. I studied it for a long moment. It was evidence enough.

At the computer, I composed what must have been my twentieth reply. This one I actually sent.

> Have you ever read about men pressing their suits overnight under mattresses back when they lived in boardinghouses and didn't have irons?
>
> Well, I have.
>
> I just found a dress I haven't worn in—get this—ten years!!
>
> It still fits. The pockets are very fruitful, if you know what I mean.
>
> Kind regards,
>
> Percy

How amazing, the way things turn up! A fundamental principle of life in any city is accumulation, but I find it holds especially true in New York, where all the open space is privatized, and one's apartment is too small. Under such conditions, things get lost. Earrings in the sink. Toothpaste in the fridge. Saltines in the teapot, because that's simply where I found them one day when I woke up. The stubborn inflow of matter collects in a terrain confined. The waste piles high in landfills, and we build over it, making land. Memories cling to every corner, shellacking Ninth Ave, until there are entire neighborhoods one feels one ought to avoid, whole shopping carts of associations to push down every street: the man who chased you across Third to grab your wrist; a green grate into which were vomited three doses of ibuprofen and the better part of a bottle of vodka from the night before; another man who looped around and around the park at Forsyth, in ridiculous circles, on your heels, complaining of the torments you'd inflicted on his heart. I will always feel a little bit with child, maybe, when I pass the 92Y. And this general sense of saturation is further exacerbated, I find, by the phenomenon of the tote, in which accrues the detritus of a day. I harnessed my caravan of canvas to the crook of my arm. There were other errands I had to run besides returning knives: I wanted to see Yvette at the hospital, Misha's presentation was that evening, there were materials to return to NYU Law. And really there is nothing so graceful as "stepping out" when your errands are so far-flung. The knives went into a tote, and half the apartment seemed to follow: papers, the self-help author's latest draft, the exhibition book, issues of *Am J Tra La*, and a copy of Misha's slides. Soon all the totes were full. I sidled down the stairs and onto the street, resolved.

I made it as far as the deli on the corner, where I ordered baklava, eggs, and toast.

The café tables were empty and lemon-scented. The man behind the counter was wiping down the meat slicer, and he watched me as I ate. I didn't mind. There was no one else there. I would have watched me, too. I looked at my plate. For weeks, Misha and I had avoided ordering cakes and baklavas. Dessert had seemed so discordant with the general mood, I'd almost forgotten how much we used to like coming here for sweets. I ordered a second baklava to bring home for him. We'd celebrate his presentation that evening, I thought, over pastries and pilaf. A new chapter would dawn in our apartment when baklavas were once again exchanged as gifts. And one could easily make a pilaf absent knives. The second pastry arrived on a square of wax paper on a thick white plate. I ate it immediately. I was like a predator, overwhelmed by a second wave of hunger. I swept a finger around the vacant dish, collecting phyllo crumbs, wishing I'd ordered three baklavas at once.

I felt ashamed about abandoning Claire. She had already been so abandoned. I should have left a note. *Be back soon! Changed my mind!* But we heartbroken people are so easily left behind. Truthfully, I was wary of Claire in the same way I imagine Constance and Yvette were wary of me, as if my woes might be contagious. I regretted accepting her invitation to knock. I hoped she'd forget. I hoped she'd sleep all day and go for a long run at night, and on those lamplit miles conclude she wanted nothing to do with me. I looked across the street at the laundromat where the self-help author had mistaken another man for Harold a month before. That life seemed quaint to me now. I missed it: wandering the neighborhood, searching for friends. Tomatoes with Misha on Saturdays, consumed whole and raw. Where had that life gone? The traces were right here, out the window, only my mother's divinations were démodé. Empirical processes were rendered impotent in the face of metaphysical moods. The only way to reassemble my life, I felt, was to confront my fiancé. All at once, it seemed I had no time to lose. Abruptly, I stood from the table and gathered my totes. Change scattered when I paid. I hurried toward the train as quickly as I could, hitched to such a load.

I had never intended for my dealings with the exhibition to go so far. But intentions are fragile things. Suddenly I was southbound, too far south, Columbus Circle was in the past. I emerged into the Garment District, turning down streets I had not walked for years. Glass buildings proliferated, as if a lid that had previously suppressed them had been lifted; they grew as diaphanous and out of place as orchids among weeds. I couldn't remember what it had looked like before. As a girl, I only ever came to the city in winter, when it was too cold to look at anything beyond the rubber toes of my boots and the grip of my mother's hand, which held mine fast as we sloshed through the snowy streets. She brought me to the ballet, for music, for jazz, plays I couldn't understand but whose sense of menace I could feel. I wonder now if she was trying to acclimatize me to that menace, vaccinate me against it, so that, later on, when I found out much of life was just a Pinter play with larger casts, worse dialogue—mere drafts of what we hoped to say—I would not be surprised. I'd been duped all the same.

Every visit requires a gift, but who knew what petty pleasures my fiancé indulged in these days? I ducked into a deli for a tin of biscuits and a box of tea, exited instead with saltines, a pot of jam, and, sheepishly, bananas. I could smell them bruising in the totes. I wished it were night. As a general rule, all that is ridiculous by day takes on a borrowed dignity after dark. Once, while standing outside a fabric dealer's on one of my late-night walks, when I was still living with my fiancé, I watched two men tumble out the exit. The larger bellowed and his friend dragged him to the curb. A woman appeared at the door to watch them go, and the bellower called after her. *When will you open again? When can we come back?* Now imagine the same scene by day. It isn't even worth retelling. This is exactly how I felt as I mounted the steps at my fiancé's. It was entirely the wrong time to arrive.

I stood at the door. Through the low windows, I could see the same armchairs and lamps—the downstairs neighbors had not left. The pink paint of the exterior was chipped, and the red of the brick showed through. I adjusted my totes, juggling knives and bananas and legal journals, like a nanny lost at noon. I didn't even know if my fiancé lived here anymore. He might have long since vanished into the city, like Harold. I looked at the buzzer and saw that it still bore his name. But a name means nothing these days. I rang. A man's steps sounded on the stairs. The door opened. It was my fiancé, in a blue sweater I had always encouraged him to wear, a blue that clashed with the pink of the house.

Of course it's you, he said.

23

Entering the pink house all these years later, it seemed too little had changed. The antique vanity in the vestibule was still flooded with menus and magazines. At the bottom of the stairwell, someone had pinned a flyer for my fiancé's show—it was probably him.

There was the feature photograph. A woman (me) lay on a bed. Smoke rose over the city skyline through the window, and moss crept along the baseboards. I did not know whether to be flattered or repelled. There was something tender and tentative about the picture. The camera's approach was silk. The shadows, demure. I nodded toward the photo.

It's like I never left.

My fiancé frowned.

Not sure I'd say that.

I followed him up five flights of steps. On the landing, he had built a shoe rack just outside the door, and here lined up three pairs of shoes. Please, he said, and I removed my own. They looked strange on the rack next to his. I looked down at my feet, disappointed to discover I'd forgotten socks.

It was strange to think that he'd been here all along. I felt I'd rather lost the capacity for staying put. And yet here he was. The apartment was far neater now than when I'd shared it with him. There was the main room, a kitchenette, the bath, the ladder that led to the loft where we used to sleep, only now the bed was in the living room. I confronted it when I came through the door.

He did not invite me to sit, and so I stayed standing in my bare feet and traveling dress, looking around the room to see what else had changed. The organization of the shoes. The clean doormat inside the door. There was a metal wine rack strung with lights, a Duchampian Christmas tree, and the walls were bare where previously there had hung prints of Schieles (mine) and his own photographs. The loft was now an atelier, judging by what I could see over the lip of the dark wooden beam: two computers glowed, and on a shelf stood an array of equipment, including an old Polaroid that I remembered well, plus a digital camera I did not. My fiancé sat on the mattress and crossed his arms. He looked up, looked away. We both glanced up at the loft.

How did you get the bed down here?

He paused.

That's right, he mused. It used to be up there.

The slanted ceiling had the effect of compressing windows on the far wall to half the usual size. Through the shrunken panes I could see the courtyard, wild and ruinous. A row of sunflowers bowed their heavy, desiccated blooms, freighted with snow. Someone had built a deck. On this sloping ceiling hung another poster from the exhibition. There she was again. Or there I was. Some version of me, asleep on the bed. The mixed response returned: revulsion and envy and also pride. I was getting used to this contradictory bouquet. It stood like a centerpiece on the mantel of my mind.

I studied my fiancé's wrists, his face. He'd grown a beard. Gained some weight. It showed in his cheeks, settled around him like a mood. I looked down the length of my own self: the traveling dress, the jacket, the daisy-showered scarf. The nebula was rising in me like a knob of dough. What a work in progress I was. I rummaged through the totes.

So you do remember me, I said.

I'm not *so* old.

I reached into the folds of my skirt for the wallet-sized photo and held it up.

He said, Who's that?

Didn't you get my email?

Yes. I'm not sure it made a lot of sense.

I went to the gallery, I said.

He nodded. I searched his face for a trace of mockery.

Those pictures, I said. They're all of me.

The corners of his eyes softened with a sadness I found persuasive. He shook his head.

Percy, he said softly. You know that that's absurd.

The trouble with that apartment, I recalled, was how difficult it always was to argue in it. I wonder if we would have made it, my fiancé and I, had we only been able to enforce, at crucial moments, some kind of separation. As things stood, there was no way to slam the door. Emotions swirled like a gas leak, diffused over the lip of the loft. We used to hurl insults from uneven altitudes, he above, I below. Then we switched, a ridiculous game of musical floors. Things often spun out of control.

I began to unpack my totes. It was something to do. I reached into an envelope with a stack of Misha's slides. *Bidding Logic: Applications of Directed Acyclic Graphs.* I discarded lipsticks and tampons and, inexplicably, a tiny silver spoon. The photographs I'd sliced were nowhere to be found. I lifted my purse and turned it upside down. Knives tumbled out—I hoped the warranty covered this kind of accident. There were fistfuls of change, coupons, legal documents, the box of tea. Bananas. Refuse rattled and came to a halt beneath the sofa. Finally the photographs sluiced from a folder. I spread them one by one across the floor, like tarot cards, in no particular order. There I was, with a book and a brush by the bed. The end table disappeared. One frame later, everything came back. Mold marched across the walls. The iterations struck me as gratuitous, verbose. There was no need to belabor it so: life was going by fast—it was careening on toward death—and I had no idea at all. I placed my hands on my hips and studied the mess. I was having trouble remembering, now, what I'd imagined producing the photos might achieve.

Outside, it had begun to rain. Through one of the windows, across the courtyard, a man appeared on the brand-new deck. The snow receded from the rails. He opened an umbrella and began to smoke. He would be able to see us, I thought. I was a veritable soap opera on dollhouse screens. I moved away, toward the doormat, knelt on the floor. I felt I might be sick. I drew in my legs and rolled my forehead against my kneecaps, the way my mother had instructed me to do whenever I felt ill. In the car she'd say, *Percy, put your head to your knees.*

My fiancé shifted on the mattress.

Look, I wouldn't have used it if I'd thought it was of you.

———

He never lied. That was part of the problem. You have to lie a little, in love, in order to get along, and he was always qualifying, cutting closer to the truth. *If we're still together* . . . I studied his stubborn face. His easy posture inside his loose blue wool. It was almost plausible, I thought, that he really had forgotten, and this struck me as worse than if he'd known. The versions of me were further proliferating. There was the woman I was with Misha, a wife who loved her husband and yet tried to kill him all the same; there was the woman in the pictures, peaceful and asleep, albeit a little bit dead; also a mother; a daughter; a somnambulist who could not sleep; and now, in addition, the woman who lived on in my fiancé's head, and who had nothing to do with the exhibition. He glanced at his watch. In the atelier, the skylight began to percuss with rain.

On the deck, the smoker crouched beneath his umbrella, relit. I glanced at Persephone, who loomed overhead. My fiancé bounced his knee. He couldn't really have forgotten, I thought. It had to be in him somewhere, the memory of me.

He stood, stretched, reached for his keys. He was stationed at the far window, looking down. I was still seated on the doormat, both hands pressed against the floor. He glanced at his watch.

It's nice to see you, Percy, but I have somewhere to be.

Let me explain.

He looked at his watch again. Then sat on the bed.

Five minutes, he said.

I took a deep breath, sank against the door. Everything slowed down. As well as I can recall, this is what I said:

TWO

The state highway that leads from the city to the small, isolated Adirondacks town where I grew up is narrow and winding and in the winter shimmers with a lacquer of black ice. You would have to be crazy or desperate to take that road in the dead of February, after dark, as my mother did one night in 1981. The way to the prison rises up through the trees, the route to New York slopes down. Traffic moves in both directions the way that loose-leaf paper floats through air, to and fro, to and fro, carving sharp corners of descent. When two cars meet, there are questions, and the truckers tend to win. The logging roads radiate in all directions, like veins from a heart, gravel seams draw gashes through the forests. There, in the distance, is the flat disc of the lake, glossed with sun. Waves of fir and pine soften the topography of hills. The road sighs through them, pedals ease, engines hiss, the lumber is silent in the trucks and softly shifting. The cool air cools further still as cords of pine, freshly felled, are guided through a leveled woods, down to the level of the lake. Brakes steam. Logs, stripped and bare, roll against the belts. The trailers begin to rock and lumber, knocking etymologies loose from the verb. The sound of dead trunks striking pavement is dull and dumb. Here is the earth unloading itself, and the road registers the rhythms that it makes. The logs settle. The landscape holds its breath and then—a new kind of silence falls, I guess, at the valley's lowest point. The road, the hill, the trees. They have no memory at all. There are only the cracks in the ice, the paths plowed through the snow. The trees fill with wind again. The birds begin to bleat.

(My fiancé shifted. He glanced at his watch.

I just want you to imagine it, I said.)

My mother often drove me to the city. I remember the low guardrails and the scent of pine and the easy splendor of the Palisades. It seems to me we were away most weekends. I didn't mind. She was a different person on the other side of the George Washington Bridge. Doors opened. Coffees came free. Trains arrived as we descended platforms and passengers gave up seats. We came, ostensibly, for museums or plays or annual ballets, but more often we simply sat in a booth in the window of a pizza parlor where she used to waitress, watching people pass. We stayed always in apartments belonging to old friends. The friends were never home, though they'd left behind perfumes, candles, frozen chickens, sets of linen drawers that slid directly into the wall. I slept beside my mother on a pull-out sofa, listening to traffic swish in the streets. I often wondered what would happen if we never left. I often wished we'd stay.

On those visits, I commanded her attention. She slipped me slices of fruit from her drinks. At home, however, I seemed not to exist for long periods of time. I lay on my back, starfished on the carpet as she vacuumed around my limbs. Rooms transformed even as I was in them. I was invisible when she cleaned the stove, polishing the burners with a dish towel. Her hair tangled and she neglected her face. She was a lover of radio and thrillers, whole worlds that bored me, and when everything was in order and to her liking, she sank into the lounge chair by the fire, opened a mystery novel, and descended into distant plots. I tried to wrench her away. I pulled all the pots from the shelves, gathered her hair into braids. Percy, she said, I'm reading. I gave up. Only in rare moments did she reveal a deep restlessness, a part of herself she rarely shared. The year before she died, she was in the habit of waking me up very late and leading me out into a night so cold we wrapped scarves around our mouths to warm the air we breathed, so as not to freeze our lungs. Once or twice we took the car in the middle of the night and drove out toward the prison, where, pulling into a clearing, she pointed to the faint stain of the Milky Way. The brief smudge of a shooting star appeared, as if someone had struck a match against the glassy surface of the sky. She brought me to the middle of the woods behind our house and here, ankle-deep in the hard crust of the snow, instructed me to remove my gloves and cup my hands around my ears, so that the whole forest came alive with sound captured in my palms. I could hear the crashing of twigs, my heart, my mother's breath, the scuttle of squirrels leaping between the branches, a cacophony that had evaded me before.

I imagine her accident as swallowed up in that sound. The call came in the deep blue of the night. My father was upstairs, asleep, as I padded from my bedroom to the phone. I had always been told my mother and I sounded alike. People confused us, and for a moment I thought that I had once again been mistaken for her. The voice on the other end spoke rapidly and with precision and did not ask if she was home, whether I could put her on. I stood there in my eyelet nightgown, phone pressed to my ear, looking out the window at the fir pine that rose thirty feet in our front yard. It was almost blue in the dark, and felled a faint shadow in the moonlight. I didn't understand. I always went to the city with my mother. What was she doing, driving alone? And why hadn't she taken me?

I'd thought a girl became her mother as a matter of course. It was predetermined. The town was small enough to throw maternal patterns into relief, and girls became predictably pretty, or obese, or ridiculed in school. I assumed it would be the same for me. But of course nothing happens automatically. You have to work at it, I find. There I was, surrounded by the raw materials of how to make a woman, how to make a home, and yet without the manuals that show how complementary parts should fit together. Only later did it occur to me assembly was a skill you had to learn. For a long time I never touched her things. Tubes of lipstick rolled solemnly in drawers. Women's coats hung in the halls. I would have told my father to put them away, I wouldn't be needing them after all, only we had no idea how to talk about what had occurred, what we referred to only as *the accident*. We hardly acknowledged she was gone, though her truancy was everywhere. The very house seemed reticent and withholding. I missed the mystery novels hanging over the backs of chairs to keep her place as she embarked half-heartedly on a list of chores. The piles of laundry she had begun but failed to sort accumulating along the baseboards. A profound silence had settled over our lives, and I realized how dependent I had been on the bizarre commotion of her housekeeping. At night I listened for my father's footsteps overhead and felt relief. I became especially attuned to his presence in the house, he less so to mine. When I crept into the living room at night, he cried out in alarm, as if he'd forgotten that he was not alone. Then the fear vanished from his face. Percy, he said. Come here. He took me in the crook of his arm.

Our town was a place of forests and lakes and federal prison compounds, a single street of shops encased in pines. A supermarket spread like a fluorescent oasis just outside district lines. We never went to the city in those years. We hardly went anywhere at all, except to the grocery or the school, or for takeout, egg rolls and lo mein. At home, the silence settled like a fog.

As if against this quiet, my father took up projects of considerable noise. That spring, when the ground thawed, he retreated to the backyard and began to build a shed. He ran a laboratory at a nearby college, and whenever he wasn't lecturing or tending to his cell cultures and slides, he could be found outside, poring over blueprints. I could hear him in the garage, training crooked planks of wood through a machine that tore through the afternoon like a departing plane. When he was through, the salvaged two-by-fours emerged straight and smooth, each identical to the next. One day a cement mixer arrived. It sat in the grass at the edge of the woods, churning heavily. My father directed the chute over four pre-drilled holes in the earth, and into these staked four naked stilts. They stood there through the summer, ready to receive a structure that so far existed only in his mind. The radio was cranked to maximum volume. News drifted. I helped by lying in the grass watching clouds. From time to time, I handed him a hammer or a wrench. I held the leveler still above the doorway, before it had been fitted with a door. My father kept calling it the woodshed—I'm going out to work on the woodshed, he'd say—but as the structure grew ever more elaborate over the following months, it dawned on me that what he was really building was a second house. That autumn a stove was installed. A crooked chimney rose through the roof. He built himself a desk. From the lab, he carried in boxes of slides and issues of *Nature* magazine, carbon-copy notebooks, spiral-bound. Then he shut himself inside. I trudged up the steps and pushed open the door. My father was seated at his freshly planed and sanded desk, preparing notes for his lecture the following day. The dog was at his feet, and when I knelt to stroke its ears, my father pulled away. I felt then how ill-equipped he was to handle me, and how much more hopeless I was, besides, to be of any help to him. I imagined us cradling puppets without the strings, a pile of joints in our arms.

When all was finished, the second house shone with lamplight through the small hours of the night. I turned onto my side, in bed, and watched the lantern of it until I fell asleep. I thought I could see my father's shadow flicker as he typed, or when he set the kettle on the woodstove for a cup of lemon tea. Although maybe he wasn't working. Maybe he was, like me, simply staring blankly out the window. In any case, I was glad to have him out there, awake. Though I missed the great orchestra of the carpentry tools, the motor of the planer in the garage, the hammering, the nails sinking into wood, the radio he played loud, streaming news from house to yard.

For my part, I watched enormous quantities of television. After dark, when my father retreated to the shed, I wandered down the hall. My mother had not believed in television. She was at her most animated when describing to me the liquefying effects it would have on my brain. There was a dolly in the coat closet, and the TV sat upon it, in her honor, hidden away. Most nights I wheeled it out from behind a wall of winter wool and into the living room, plugged it in. There, on my belly before the woodstove in the main house, I flipped through the channels. I fell asleep to sitcom laughter of vague, off-screen origins, watched women latch gold chains. I was obsessed for a time with *Wheel of Fortune*. The tiles of the spinner glittered, hypnotic in the dark. It didn't really matter to me what was on. What mattered was that I could imagine myself as one in a crowd, that the same scenes unfolded in distant living rooms just as they did in mine.

I watched until the sky began to blush. I went on walks at dawn through the woods, skidded stones across the icy surface of the pond. I was spotted strolling through the snow on my own at odd hours, pausing for long moments to cup my ears, collecting sounds. There had always been some concern, among my teachers and the parents of my friends, that I was not getting on as well as I might. Certain traits were becoming more pronounced. She was just standing there, a neighbor said. I thought she was a deer. Imagine if I'd shot.

The previous owner of our house had also hunted deer, and in the high branches of the prodigious pine in our front yard remained a platform where he used to aim his bow. I could see it from the ground. One day, I decided to climb to it. I was curious how far one could see from that apartment in the pine. Probably not so far. Not to the city, maybe. But why not try? The branches began low to the earth, a few inches above the rust bed of the needles, and I notched my boots against the bark. It was winter and the air was blue with cold. The mountains blurred with frost. The sun came up. When I looked down, I saw the twin houses, icicles descending in a glimmer from the eaves. I made it to the platform and kept climbing. It was an old tree, a grandfather tree past its prime, and my mother was often saying how beautiful it was. I thought of it as a friend. I secured my boot into a final foothold and reached. The branch fell, and I followed it to the ground.

The doctors said it was the fresh snow that saved me. The breathing machine had something to do with it, too. I woke up in the hospital to find tubes snaking from my nose and chest. The doctors appeared at my bedside to explain things calmly and thoroughly, as if the better informed I was, the more likely I would be to recover. A pneumothorax, I learned, is the collapsing of that fragile purse inside the chest, and though in theory one can live quite normally with a single lung, one's energy for life is consequently halved. The question was whether my conquered organ, flattened by the impact of my fall, would reinflate on its own. For a week, I breathed with help. Then I sank into a deep sleep as they sent a second scalpel between my ribs. After, a nurse came in to test my strength. She placed the mouthpiece of a large plastic pump between my teeth and commanded me to breathe. My rehabilitated lung complied, and she sent me home. At night, my father sat on the edge of my bed as I performed my exercises. He propped me up on pillows as I breathed into a balloon that measured the force my exhalation produced. He stood for a long moment in the dark and placed a palm on my head. Please, please, he said. Don't do stupid things like that again.

(My fiancé looked out the window.

Did you ever find out where your mother went?

I shook my head.

You were lucky.

Yes, I said.)

We'd hardly left town since the accident. Once we went to Montreal, to buy a winter coat. Other than that, I went no farther than I could ski or bike. I cycled to the café on Main Street in the afternoons, where I poured endless sugar packets into coffee, or to the highway, the entrance to the ski resort. Then I turned around and traced the same path home. My world had become smaller. It was my mother who'd taken me to the World Trade Center and the Met, the corner of Twenty-Third and Tenth, and other places that held for her some power. My father resented the city. It wasn't until I was older, and had my license, that my range of reference began to expand.

There is a certain kind of freedom in neglect. I went where I could, whenever I pleased, and I had to thank my father for that. He taught me how to drive. When I was fifteen, he took me to the supermarket after hours to turn slow laps around the lot. It wasn't immediately intuitive to me, which pedal referred to the gas, and which to the brake, and on those first few voyages I upturned a trash can or two. My father wasn't fazed. That's all right, he said. That's why we came so late, no one's around. I was grateful. He settled into the passenger seat, his breath rising in slow clouds, popped a tape into the cassette, and turned the volume loud. I imagine you would have been able to hear us from the freezer section of the empty store as I drew endless circles around the lot, passing dumpsters, streetlights, the pines that crept to the pavement's edge, all the while broadcasting the muffled melodies of Bob Marley and the Who. We made an eerie scene, I'm sure, traversing our ghost rounds after midnight. In the end, I learned to parallel-park between two dumpsters, two cones, two bike racks my father had drawn together for a challenge. The first thaw, I woke very early, took the keys from the hook, and eased the Volvo over the GWB, just as my mother used to do.

I was not very adventurous or bold, and had no money. I visited the places I had gone with her. The ballet. The Met, where there was a new painting I did not particularly like but which stuck in my mind all the same. It was there in the gallery that used to host the bather series, in which blurry women climb in and out of tubs, comb hair, dry the webbing between their toes, and otherwise perform those acts that women do when they imagine themselves to be alone. Only that day the bathers were gone, and in their place hung this small portrait of a man. He was a Russian author, I read, who'd thrown himself down the stairs. It was true that in the picture he had a tragic air. He hung between two self-portraits of an Impressionist and was seated at a writing desk. Steel winter light streamed through the pale window. I wondered if he'd managed to maintain that expression of despair for the entire sitting, or whether the portraitist had captured it all at once, in an instant. I knelt so I was level with the object label. I thought, I'd never choose the stairs.

(You can't have thought that at sixteen.

Well, I'm thinking it now.)

I made periodic trips to the city in those years. I'm not entirely sure my father knew where I was. He was in the lab, or the garage, hunched over the planing machine. When I was home he knocked on my door to ask how was school, what was I reading, would I like an egg? He served them soft-boiled, in little cups, dish towel folded pedantically over his shoulder. It was no surprise, when it came time to apply for college, that I chose the one farthest from home and closest to the city, which in the end was not so far. My father drove. I looked out the window, where the landscape grew flush and green and neat, as it always did when we crossed state lines. Most places seemed better off. The campus stretched dully in every direction. There were cupolas and tympanums and lawns that would take all day to mow, I knew, because that had been my job at home. My father helped to unload my things and drew me close. I walked to the registration hall and selected the classes he'd suggested I take. Then I returned to the dorm, lay down in the single bed, and fell asleep.

I was still there when my roommate arrived. The door swung open, and a girl appeared. She stood with her suitcase and a set of boxes, her long dark hair plastered to her cheeks with sweat. At the sight of me, she pushed it back behind her ears. Hi, I said. She looked around the empty room. How long have you been here? I told her I wasn't sure. She nodded. I'm Yvette. I propped myself on the mattress to shake her hand. I think I'll unpack now, she said. She was brisk. The boxes opened, her clothes disappeared neatly into drawers. She hung posters and strings of lights. I hadn't brought any photographs or ornaments. I had with me a shoebox of notes, a few mystery novels, a fistful of pencils my father had sealed in an empty coffee tin. When Yvette ran out of space to hang her memorabilia and prints, I let her decorate my walls, too. Pictures caked the closet doors. She hung a paper lantern. Above my bed, a map of the city appeared. That semester, when I could not sleep, I lay awake charting tedious routes from Harlem, down Manhattan, into Queens.

I came to rely on Yvette. She'd grown up in the city, Upper East, and if there was ever a question as to who should lead our party of two, the answer was Yvette. The logic of the campus lay just beyond my grasp. I could feel that it was there, like a cliff edge in the dark, only, unlike a precipice, it did not after a series of calculated steps reveal itself to me. Instead I took my cues from her. I borrowed her clothes. I peered at her notes during lectures, to see if what we'd written was the same. One day, in the cafeteria, as we slid along the buffet line, I found myself mindlessly spooning the same foods onto my plate. Yvette paused. You don't even like polenta. I looked at it, confused. I know I don't, I said.

At home, my father had taken to reading the mystery novels that had once so captured the attention of my mother. They rose in a tower beside the armchair when I came home for winter break. He summarized them for me in long monologues delivered over the phone. He loved Agatha Christie, the intrigues of the landed gentry, anything about the Orient Express. The local library was very small, and I worried sometimes he'd run out. What would he do with his evenings then? I wandered through the stacks at school, selecting every thriller I could find, packed them into cereal boxes, and shipped the whole lot home. I called to check in. Thank you, Percy, my father said. He reminded me to focus on my grades. It struck me as unfair, sometimes, that life had turned out this way.

After a holiday at home, where the mountains ran along the horizon in every direction, encircling the town, there was something about the campus that struck me as fake, like decorative garden rocks made out of foam. I didn't trust it, and so, while I enjoyed attending lectures, I couldn't bring myself to worry about where it was all supposed to lead. I was just intelligent enough to know that I was not especially smart, and this made it difficult to take my own schooling seriously. I looked around my linear algebra class and saw everyone taking notes with an urgency I could not muster. I turned to look out the window, where the first snow blurred, and wondered why I'd come to college at all. My mother had no degree. Yvette was skeptical of this line of thought. Percy, she said. At least you have to try. Alone at a carrel in the science library, I set up a Taylor series to determine the diminishing returns of a distant star's pull on the earth. I studied the refractive bend of an Einsteinian lens, a perspectival trick produced by the celestial roadblock of a black hole, and which multiplies one star into many. I calculated base ratios of oxygen to nitrogen for organic reactions measured out in moles. Only I had internalized some fear of the body. I was afraid sometimes that mine would give way. That I would faint, or my weak lung would collapse, or my limbs act on one of the irreversible and ridiculous thoughts that frequently crossed my mind. There are moments in life when I feel the immediate future is not an experience to be lived but rather a solid object to admire or try on, like a shirt on a hanger a saleswoman holds up, saying, This would look nice on you. I tried on summer, tomorrow, one minute from now, to see if they might suit. At night, atop the astronomy building, powerful lasers made illusory points of reference on the dome of the night. I looked over the edge of the roof and simultaneously willed and resisted the urge to fall. I could feel something in me brace, like two hands about to shove. There was a sensation of pushing, leaping, and also the awareness that I stood still on a Cartesian plane. I had not jumped, I was walking across the frozen lawn to the dining hall. In our dorm, I changed into a sweater. I brushed my hair. What's that? Yvette said. I lowered my gaze to the small scars beneath my arm. I was being stupid, I said.

I sat at my desk and tried to concentrate. It was no use. I'm afraid my primary preoccupations were imagining a dive off the roof of the astronomy building, the menu for dinner, the general humiliation of being eighteen. Because few things are as dispiriting, I find, as being contradicted ad infinitum. My father, surfacing from his whodunit, disagreed.

That spring, I landed myself in the art history building, where we were learning about the relationship of parts to whole, background to foreground. I settled into a seat. Disparate planes snapped together on a nylon projector screen. The result was a productive tension. The paintings were unstable even as they were whole. I was introduced to Mondrian. Black lines laid themselves across a blank white plane. They crossed at perpendicular junctures, sectioning the painting into small squares of white, blue, red, or yellow, and this layering of borders, pigments, the banality of the plane, made it difficult to see in the end, the professor said, which was the subject and which was the support. Was this a lattice of lines overlaid, or white squares painted on a sheet of solid black? Or did the foundation of the painting exist primarily as a variegated outcrop of red, yellow, blue that the white squares, the black lines, eclipsed? It was impossible to tell. And because you couldn't tell, the professor said, you continued to search, such that the viewer remains within the painting. The composition holds her gaze as the eye cycles through the iterations. First the lattice of lines floats into the foreground, then the primary colors, the canvas itself. The hierarchy of the planes is perpetually revised, and it is the constant motion that makes it whole. The disruption itself is the most stable thing. The professor clicked the remote. New slide.

This kind of reasoning felt extremely important to me. For a while, I, too, became an idealist, not unlike Mondrian. I shifted my life into these new rooms. The atmosphere was far superior to the dour auditoriums in which I was taught chemistry and math. The sting of fresh paint was sharp in the halls. Classes convened pleasantly in the sun-soaked galleries of the museum. I stayed. I found it an immediate relief to know that whatever we were learning was not especially applicable to the outside world. On a Tuesday afternoon, we waded through the hermeneutics of being-here versus being-for-ourselves, resisted being-for-others, though we always were a little bit. We were here for ourselves and others all at once. That was the tragedy, I supposed. Although it seemed the less one knew, the less certain one was, the less one ran the risk of sounding stupid. For once I even felt a little smart. I knew nothing about the arts, and it proved better to understand nothing of Dasein than to internalize but half. My professors, disinterestedly contemplating manifolds, graded leniently. I had a knack for disinterested contemplation myself. I saw Yvette a little less. One day, over lunch, our trays lined up edge to edge, she said, Maybe I should take art. I watched a cardinal land on a pliable branch out the window. The limb bobbed with the red weight of the bird. Sure, I said. I was relieved, when it came time to register for classes, that she chose electromagnetism instead.

The way you worked through the problem of a painting wasn't so different, in the end, from the way you addressed a problem in math, or in life. Or at least the way I did. Crudely torn squares of paper fell randomly to pale blue and there were glued in place. Three standard stoppages, measured by meter-length strings and dropped from some height, were subsequently carved in wood. Of all the possible permutations, why should this be the one that wound up in MoMA, under glass? In curatorial studies, we examined the voice that emanated directly from gallery walls. How should a work be presented and described, assuming it should be described at all? It was the one space I had away from Yvette where I felt at peace, even if it was a world bent on critiquing itself into oblivion, its status obsolete.

One semester, I led a discussion section for the professor who'd taught us how to view a Mondrian. I stood dutifully in the front of the room, my palms yellow with chalk. The students, it turned out, did not at all share the assigned reading's enthusiasm for the arts, irreproducible or otherwise. Honestly, someone said, the more difficult something is to read, the less I want to read it. Others nodded. A young man stabbed his finger into the pages piled on his desk and proclaimed, This guy writes like a dick. A mathematical boy in glasses, who I knew for a fact was capable of higher-order thinking, raised his hand. I don't get the aura, he said. I asked if someone else might be so kind as to explain. A sophomore in sailor stripes made a valiant effort, relying heavily on gesticulations with her hands. It's like how when you see the David, she said, it's just *there*. Like— *oomph*. She brought a fist to the center of her chest for emphasis. The class stared blankly. I myself hadn't been to Florence, so I was reluctant to weigh in. Sounds a lot like nostalgia to me, the thin, bespectacled student said, proving he was capable indeed. That isn't an argument at all. It might be more useful, I suggested, to take on the idea of authenticity. Together we considered the painting versus the print. The print of a painting has a referent hanging somewhere in the Louvre, I said. But then take the film. It's manipulated and spliced. Its actual making exists nowhere but in the minds of those who performed the many disparate takes, spread across many days. Therefore, the film didn't *re*-present anything. It was its own representation of itself. And yet, for this reason it was the least authentic genre of all, for the film aims to appear what it decidedly is not, a natural, cohesive, uninterrupted whole, a continuous stretch of time. There was a silence in the room. I jotted some notes on the board. A precocious freshman lifted her cheek from her hand. So it's kind of like memory? I looked at her. Yes, exactly like that.

My father had grown bitter, living in two separate houses on his own, surrounded by stacks of books he'd already read, mysteries he'd already solved. Come home soon, he said, when I called a month or so before my graduation. He suggested I get a job in the lab. I could still retrain. It wasn't too late, he'd teach me himself. All right, I said. Then I hung up the phone. I looked at the receiver on my desk. I hadn't known how badly I did not want to return to those silent rooms, the woodstove, the glow of the old TV, until my father suggested it.

It was May, and the blackflies had arrived. When I reached beneath my hair, a scab sloughed off neatly in my nail. The whole school was outside, languid, as if struck dead in the grass. I wandered across campus to the library, which was silent and empty and cool. The windows above the thesis carrels were stuffed with air-conditioning units, and the whole space hummed. At a computer terminal, I logged on to search a database of jobs. In the entry for "major," I typed "art." I could be a teacher, the computer offered.

Only I didn't really enjoy standing in front of a crowd. Before an audience, I lost my way. I searched again. The database suggested ventures in culture, diplomacy, interior decorating, and, inexplicably, the FBI. I clicked the help button, and a dialog box appeared. It asked how it could be of service. I wanted to know what it was my experiences had prepared me for, and whether, in the event I did not like those options, it was too late to become someone else.

I drifted across the lawn toward the art and architecture building in the hope that my advisor was in. I couldn't say why this professor had taken such an interest in me. He had hired me as his assistant, offered me a campus job, generally treated and graded me generously. Once or twice, I'd babysat his children. He lived in a small white house in town with a trampoline in the yard, and I spent the evening considering my level of responsibility should one of his sons leap and, with the compact mass of his small body, draw a perfect arc across the lawn. It's possible I might have shown some aptitude for research, or at least for babysitting, managing a discussion section he did not have time to lead. In each of these departments, however, I was sure that I was average. I stood in the door to his office now, wondering what it was he had seen in me, and whether it was monetizable in any way.

I knocked. Come in, he said. I settled into the chair across from his desk. The office was lined with hundreds of books, and above the shelves hung a framed print of *Les Demoiselles d'Avignon*. So, Percy. What can I do for you? It was a good question, one that had seemed much easier to answer while I was still outside waiting in the hall. I sat in silence. Then I laid out my conundrum. I did not have a job, I said, and after graduation it was impossible to go home. My professor nodded. I was very grateful that he did not ask me to expand. I see, he said. Well, is there anything you'd like to do? I noticed his books were organized chronologically rather than alphabetically, according to developments in painting through time. I looked at my hands. Maybe I'd like to work in a museum, I said. Or an archive. Anywhere, really, that was not my father's lab. My professor nodded again. Then he reached for his phone. When he hung up, I had officially applied and been hired for a temporary position at a small East Side gallery devoted to Himalayan art, not so far from Yvette's apartment, and for which I was grossly underqualified.

(My fiancé frowned.

I don't think I ever met Yvette.

Of course you did, I said.)

It isn't easy to find a room. The summer after I graduated, I spent a number of weeks living with Yvette and her mother. It was a temporary arrangement that lasted longer, I think, than anyone had planned. Her bedroom was dark green, and through the upper pane of the windows I could see the tops of smokestacks rising over Queens. We sat together in the kitchen reviewing flashcards for her matriculation to medical school that fall. Yvette liked to plan ahead. The apartment was very still and silent, with long, pale halls, and fans in every room, to aid the passage of cigarette smoke out the open windows. Her mother was the smoker. She was retired, and she swept through those halls all day in a robe, trailing ash, retracing the same path from kitchen to parlor to her bedroom, where she spent her afternoons at a desk, typing up her memoirs. The dark steel of her bedspread echoed the power plant out the window. Our own room was sweltering, and at night I lay awake in Yvette's trundle, level with the floor, legs arranged to catch the current of the air conditioner. It was too hot to sleep. My father's warnings had followed me. The city was expensive and difficult, he'd said, and what would I do when my internship came to an end, armed with only the blunt instrument of an art history major? I lived in sustained fear of wearing out my welcome. For a while I kept a jar of peanut butter and a bag of bread in the cupboard and ate mostly that. I made PB&Js standing up, jar wedged beneath my arm. What is she doing? Yvette's mother whispered, addressing her daughter and looking at me. Percy, Yvette said. Don't be ridiculous. Of course you'll eat with us.

The gallery was on Second Avenue, a twenty-minute walk. I had my own key and was often there alone all day. There was no one around to tell me to leave after closing up, and so sometimes I just stayed. I locked the door and took a turn through the displays. I slipped on a sixteenth-century pendant made of jade, lowering the necklace onto my chest the way I'd seen in infomercials, where faceless women were adorned by disembodied hands. I took walks through the semi-deserted blocks, pausing at the eastern edge of Turtle Bay to watch traffic accumulating on the FDR. I stopped in bodegas for buttered bagels. Bouquets of flowers grouped, wilting, in green bins, begging to be bought. I chose some for myself. I carried them back through the last of the night, just as the first commuters began to appear. Back on Second Ave, I glided seven floors to the reception area, arranged the coterie of gladioli in an ancient vase. Then I folded my arms at the kidney-shaped desk and fell asleep.

The showroom was installed in one of those old buildings favored by offices of the estates of the deceased, dentists, acupuncturists. A directory referred visitors to one of nine floors, each littered with LLCs. The elevator creaked. I opened a broom closet and out fell a dermatologist's lamp. I shoved it back inside. From the reception area in the mornings, when I lifted my head and rubbed my eyes, I had a view of the avenue and glass cases filled with rare objects of Himalayan origin in which the gallery specialized. My job was to sit at the desk and answer a phone that almost never rang. Occasionally I showed a potential buyer the sixteenth-century pendant, a gongshi evocative of a human face. I wrote an auction label for a copper bodhisattva, deftly seated, one divine palm turned outward in a sign of blessing. I hosted general visitors with no intention to buy. They were intrepid characters who came in from the street, European tourists in backpacks and sneakers who'd already exhausted the museums along the park. They wandered through the room, whispering, pleased to have found the gallery at all. We had recently acquired panels from an elaborate Tibetan almanac, quite rare, and, relying heavily on the text on the wall, I helped my guests uncover the animal and element corresponding to the year in which they were born. How hungry everyone was for the exegesis of herself. They were pessimistic and empathetic and shy. They ought to avoid poor weather and dangerous sports. I myself didn't want to know what 1989 had in store. Though I took preemptive measures to shore up luck. There was a prayer wheel installed in the corner, fixed atop a large armoire, and when I was alone in the gallery, after the European tourists and speculators had cleared, I stood on a stool to reach the red wheel and delivered a single turn. The Sanskrit slid by inscrutably. I spun it again. I wondered if these recitations still counted, karmically, if I could not grasp conceptually the prayer that I had made.

The owner was an infrequent presence. When she did stop by, it was usually to replenish a bowl of pomegranates that sat on the large dining table in the frontmost room. Her daughter lived in California, on a plot with bumper crop, and she was always sending more. If I eat another I'll be sick, she said. The sanguine fruits poured from a paper bag. I was tasked with disposing of the old batch in the dumpster downstairs. I can still smell the sweet-rot of the bulbs, hear the faint wet thud the small globes made, so reminiscent of flesh, falling into the bin. After, I washed the copper bowl in the sink and set it, gleaming and empty, in its place on the oblong table. It was never long before the gallerist appeared with a new shipment and braced a razor blade against the thick seams of tape. Christ, she packs these like cocaine, she said. The seal tore, and twenty or thirty new pomegranates tumbled forth. I started bringing them home to Yvette's, where we made pomegranate cakes, juices, jams.

Yvette and her mother were wonderful friends, I thought. They screamed and slammed doors. I sat in the kitchen with a bowl of cereal, listening to them argue. They shouted down the corkboard halls. Later, Yvette peeled an onion to help her mother make a sauce. She borrowed and ruined lipstick. Again they fought. I had never argued so violently with anyone in my life, not even Yvette. I was too afraid that if I did, then I really would be sent away. That Yvette's mother could condescend her choice in clothes as we sidled out the door on Saturdays seemed to me evidence of a profound trust I did not recognize in my own life. When my father and I were angry with each other, he retreated across the yard, and I rolled the television set from the coat closet. There was no arguing with my father's decisions. We waited out his anger like a storm. At the edge of our relationship there lay a sudden drop, and I was careful not to plunge.

In the fall, when Yvette moved away for school, her mother and I sat alone in the kitchen in the evenings, exerting a quiet influence on each other. She took up peanut butter sandwiches. I took up smoking. On weekends, we clipped coupons, and they fluttered to the floor, forming coded recipes derived from weekly deals. Ritz, cheddar, Chicken of the Sea. Together, they alluded to a discount tuna melt. I looked around at the place I'd come to think of as a home. The floors were slick and shone. Lemons gathered in a bowl. Teacups hung on silver hooks above two stainless cake stands. It pained me that Yvette's mother and I had so much more trouble talking now that her daughter was gone. My position at the gallery was expiring soon, and late at night, when I came home, I sat in the kitchen by the lemon bowl and wrote and rewrote applications. Yvette's mother juiced a lemon into a water glass—for her skin, she said—and asked me about my day, how was work, what I was thinking of doing next. I juiced a lemon, too. I don't really know, I said. It was distressing how difficult I found answering these questions. I stayed up, thinking, after she retired to her room.

One night, the chatter of the typewriter paused. I listened for the sound of slippers in the hall. Yvette's mother appeared, offered me a cigarette. Thanks, I said. I was at my usual spot at the table, staring blankly at a page, surrounded by coupons and abandoned cover letters. I was having little luck finding another job. She filled the kettle, took two teacups from their hooks. As we waited for the chamomile to steep, she considered the résumés strewn across the floor and frowned. Let me see what I can do.

Quite a lot, it turned out. She knew someone at the French Embassy, who knew someone in a downtown gallery, who knew yet another woman capable of pulling strings at the art auction house in Midtown, which was in need of copy editors. I hadn't realized nepotism had so long a reach. I soon found myself at a desk in Rockefeller Plaza, alongside the likes of Constance. For one final week, Yvette's mother and I composed an awkward duet in that kitchen, trading cigarettes and peanut butter knives. I didn't have the words to express my gratitude. The morning I left, I placed a note by the lemon bowl that had taken me all night to draft. *Thank you so much*, it read. *I have never felt so at home.*

(You should have stayed in touch.

But I did, you know that.)

There is a particular persona to adopt when writing text for galleries or the pages of an auction magazine. I suppose I had it. It was rather my natural state to present the subjective as a kind of universal truth. Or else I didn't have such a strong definition of my own subjectivity to start, so it wasn't hard to set it aside. Borrowed authority is easy to perform. Upstairs, at the risk analysis firm, you saw things the other way around. Simple truths were always qualified with doubt.

The first day, at the elevator bank:

After you.

The second:

You again.

The third, the fourth:

You don't talk much, do you?

The fifth:

If I were being forward, I'd give you my card.

I should have known, as you already knew, how stories that begin this way tend to end.

I can be slow, my reactions delayed, but I was no simpleton. I should have known, I knew.

At the time, however, the outcome had not seemed so certain. Over dinner, you explained. In any scenario, p was the chance that something terrible would come to pass, and q was the status quo. The coin flipped day to day. I was all for disruption back then. But look at you now. I suppose I'm the one who stayed the same.

My new room was in Brooklyn, in an apartment filled with

samovars and first-edition books. The room itself was very red and small, and I'd rented it because the owner, Mme Popov, often went home to the Soviet Union to visit her mother for weeks at a time. It's Latvia, she said. I thought when she left that I would have the apartment to myself. It was true that she was often gone. What I had not anticipated, however, was that other women would come to take her place. Madame used the extra rent to fund her flights. It was not such a lie when I told you the apartment was chaotic, you ought not to come. I was more afraid, however, that you might choose one of the women I lived with instead, if only you had the opportunity to meet them. The roommates rotated. A ballerina, a medical student, an actress who smoked more than she ate and yet who was always delving into cupboards and leaving dishes in the sink, where the roaches skittered. The only common theme among them was that they all relied on me. I was temporary super of the fourth floor. The pipes froze, the heat sputtered, someone smashed the glass. It was curious that these things happened only when Mme Popov was gone, as if her very presence kept the building secure, temperate, and pumping steam. The women who came to stay in her stead looked to me for guidance, to kill the roaches, to call the actual super about restoring hot water to the faucet, as if I were in charge. I didn't feel in charge at all. And yet, I was always reminding the actress, especially, to be more careful about leaving food and soiled plates and teacups on the counters. I left notes on cupboard doors. *No dirty dishes in the sink! No ashtrays on the books!* After a while I started smoking inside, too, and ashed onto the Nabokovs.

I was spending less and less time in my red room. I was always out, on a roof, at a movie with you. I was living the life I imagined the women I worked with had when they left the office at half past five. Who needed the internet when I had your brain nearby? I queried and you replied. You knew more about everything, and if there was ever a disagreement, I was quick to yield. I gave up ground on geography, calculating tips, on match girls from Vienna—I hadn't realized those nudes had been so shrilly sketched. The only area in which I excelled was in remembering things you didn't. Walking past Penn Station, along the high steps of the post office, I recalled the fight we'd had outside the DMV. The old Malaysian place was now a French café. I was good at knowing when things would disappear. I liked to guess who people were, the relationships between them. On the train, a father and son were lovers instead, when the young man put a hand on the elder's knee and asked, Which one is our stop again?

I wonder if I was relieved, in a way, to be told what to do. At Mme Popov's, I was the authority in the room. The actress was in many respects even less equipped to handle life than I, and I could never decide whether my primary reaction to this was superiority or envy. When she asked me questions about how she ought to live her life, with all the sincerity of a child, as if certain I would know the answer, I felt wise. Then again, the options she had to choose among were always so glamorous, it was hard not to wish that they were mine. She yelled from the bathroom one night, This man on the subway gave me his card! Should I call him up? She appeared in the door and leaned against the jamb, sank a curling iron into her hair. Only there's a casting party, she said. I was at the table, eating toast. The clamp released, a buoyant spiral fell. I watched its celebratory bounce. Percy, she said. What to do with myself?

Her room was at the opposite end of the apartment, and we slept separated by the tiny kitchen and the jacquard chaise, over which she stepped each morning, bare knees parting a yellow silk robe. She undressed while in the vestibule, depositing coat and skirt and boots in a pile in the hall. Once inside, she never wore anything but that yellow robe. Standing on the kitchen tiles, drinking coffee, she reached into a pocket and produced a second pair of panties, held them to her waist. Should I wear these? she asked. Or these? She was invested in her undergarments. Those, I said. She nodded. I think that's right. It was around this time, as I showered the actress with simple advice, that I began to wonder about my conversations with you. It wasn't statistically sound, for me to be wrong all the time.

The problem with seeing someone so much older than you is that memory flows in only one direction. I liked to hear how the city had changed, how everything was twenty years ago. As the younger party, however, it was always better if I had no past, no parents, no dramas outside of you. No trouble finding a room, for example, or another place to stay. If I interrupted a Tuesday movie, pressed pause on the VCR to call my father, you seemed surprised. It was as if you'd forgotten I'd had one all this time. I took the phone into the bathroom and shut the door. My father was growing more eccentric by the day. He had four dogs now, a greenhouse in which to nurture cultures, curate slides. He'd built an annex to the shed. The pine in the front yard, he said, had caught a fungus, and the trunk was compromised. He'd have to cut it down. Was he sure? He was. It was a hazard. It might come crashing onto the roof, the car. Already it had nearly killed at least one of us. I implored him to get a second opinion, but my father had made up his mind. I loved that tree. I hung up in a gloom. No one is ever listening to me, I said, once I was sure that no one was.

(My fiancé sighed.

I'm sure that's not true.)

I followed the actress to parties. I wore her clothes. A skirt. Her boots. I let her curl my hair. Occasionally I exchanged numbers with someone more my age. I followed people home, where we sat silently on sofas. There wasn't ever much to say. This was not the place for arguments about art, preferences for Caravaggio over Raphael. The man I was with never did care to pick apart my reasoning with respect to Schiele versus Klimt. I drew out the conversation, parroting opinions, until that moment he kissed me abruptly, wetly, pressed play. The sequence of events was always the same, and I was always surprised. Once supine, I realized I hadn't thought things through this far. I was reminded of my father's planing machine, into which he fed and shaped a crooked wooden board. My mind wandered. I was complacent and still. Though there was a struggle from time to time. One night I fell asleep. When I woke up, the man whose bed I was borrowing was plying away, shoving himself in. Extracting, I suppose, what he was due in rent. I pushed, elbowed, applied my fists. He pinned. What a trick! Through some acrobatics, I maneuvered away. There was a quiet moment in which we both attempted to make sense of what had just occurred. I reached through the dark, feeling for my bra and the actress's shirt. Then I stood and straightened my clothes. I have to go, I said. He looked at me a moment, suddenly harmless, sheepish. He offered to walk me to the train. That's okay, I said.

You were always taking pictures. The shutter snapped at the post office, in the deli, as I was coming out of the shower, wreathed in steam. I never liked to be in pictures, though I liked that you were looking at me. What a composition I would have made that night, waiting for the subway! My reflection was stark in the window of the train. I looked away. At home, the apartment felt unusually silent. The actress was out. I scraped a dusting of cocaine from the table with a Playbill and threw everything away. I slipped on her robe. I looked into a cookbook, into the fridge at a half carton of eggs, and contemplated making a soufflé. Instead I washed all the dishes in the sink. Ran a bath. The actress's silk pooled on the floor. Through the narrow window, I caught a sliver of the sky. I brought the phone into the tub and sat with it a moment. Then I dialed.

If we're still together, I said, could you come over right now?

That was the one time you came to my red room. The windows were cracked, and winter came through. The Chrysler Building rose over the sill. The apartment reeked of cabbage and parsnip and other kinds of soup that the actress, in her lower moods, had learned to make. I remember I was pleased to have you, finally, in my bed instead of yours. I turned off the lights. In the morning, I woke up alone.

The phone rang.

Let's not see other people anymore.

There are any number of arguments that last a lifetime. Ours was simple enough. Which one of us was right? I suppose differences in taste in art transpose to different tastes in life. One day, not long after I moved in, on the steps of the Met I pointed out an especially beautiful couple standing silently side by side. He was tall and dark and thin. She was in heels and the darker mood. We were on our way to see a photography exhibit, photography-cum-architecture, or pictures of parts of a house. Only I was transfixed by this scene outside. Look, I said, still standing on the steps. They're splitting up. Can't you tell? You always were reluctant to pass judgment on a work in progress. On this one point, however, it felt important to hold my ground, and soon we were having an argument ourselves. You turned to go into the museum. I stayed on the steps. I looked toward the fountain. The woman was now walking away, as fast as one can in heels through the Saturday crowds.

Then the man ran after her, caught her in an embrace. She accepted it stiffly, arms at her sides.

Considering only the parts of things, I think, will make you feel sad. That day, after the small scene on the steps, we drifted through the exhibition, apologetic. There was little to say about the parceled roofs and porches and split-level homes split further between two frames. I was the first to break the silence. I said, I have a new favorite painting. I led us through sculpture, through landscapes, past the series of bathers, in which the wet curves of a woman are tinged with green, past the many variations on la coiffure, of older women tugging a younger woman's hair over the back of a wooden chair, ready to comb, to cut. I was looking for the portrait of the Russian author who'd thrown himself down the stairs, but when we arrived at the corner where I expected him to be, it appeared he'd fled. Instead we stood in front of Mäda Primavesi. She poses in an addled room, fat flowers floating in the background. The perspective is wrong. The walls threaten to fold into a horizontal line. The placard states that at the time of painting the girl was eight, but with her direct stare and solid stance, Mäda could be twenty. For all I know she could be hiding a knife in her drop-waist tulle. These days I prefer paintings whose subjects, were they ever to escape from the picture plane, seem less likely to wreak havoc. That is a concession I can make. That there is something noble in the rigor of balance and design. In standing still for extended periods of time. I admired all those women who posed, who only pretended to step into a bath. Arms straining, they held their own weight. It takes a long time to make a painting. One ought to take breaks.

I suppose it was a little late for me to begin thinking in ifs. I no longer had a room of my own. I'd moved in with you. I pressed pause on the VCR. You stiffened. I always had to call my father,

I did so once a week, and still it always came as a surprise. One night I lost heart. You were in the middle of explaining Hollywood production codes, according to which du Maurier's novel had been adapted for the screen. I looked at the phone in my hand. At Joan Fontaine, frozen mid-scene. I always found it difficult to straddle two worlds at once. I'm experiencing an absence of confidence, I said, about what we want. Percy, you replied, that's absurd.

How nice to have production codes! In Hollywood a spousal murderer never goes unpunished. Every narrative must follow the rule. There are too many possibilities otherwise. One has to keep from living all of them at once. I had no plans. At the same time, I packed a bag. I kept it in the closet. I found an apartment, signed a lease. Also organized a wedding. I stood for a long moment at the top of the stairs, contemplating my descent. I'm going out for a walk, I yelled. Where to? you asked. I shouldered my duffel bag. I did not consider the p's or q's of what might happen next. On this side of the screen, I think, most things come down to timing and proximity, to chance. One claims credit where one can and tries not to die ashamed. I walked three miles north. The sky threatened snow. In Morningside, the landlord met me at the door to hand off the keys. He pointed inside at the phone, rolled his eyes. It's for you, he said. And again with timing and proximity! I should have answered. But I was busy, I was moving in. No matter that there was hardly anything to unpack. The phone rang again, and again. Except I was already in bed, the cordless was across the room. And besides, I didn't know what to say.

(You could have gotten an answering machine.

The guy at RadioShack told me they were already becoming obsolete.)

The apartment was empty, silent, neat. There were no roaches, no boarders, nothing in my room but a mattress on the floor. It felt clean. I made toast and instant coffee. Downstairs, at a neighbor's, I watched hospital dramas on TV. I called Yvette. For once, she did not try to counsel me, ask questions, say I was making a mistake. She told me it was all right not to know what I wanted, all right to take my time. I said the same to you, I need a little time. I was taking a moment to think things over. That was all. I'd hardly brought anything, the closets were empty, I went to East End Avenue to borrow clothes. I arrived late for work in Yvette's dresses and slacks, outfits that no longer fit her and which she'd left behind. I wore her skirts, too snug. When my colleagues asked me why my object labels were late, I said I didn't know. Maybe I was becoming sentimental. Only, there was no time for sentiment. The inventory for the auction had already arrived, and buyers needed guidance from the catalog. I couldn't concentrate, however. You were just upstairs. I could have heard you if you'd stomped.

I wasn't planning to quit on the day that I did. I woke up with a large bruise. I'd fallen asleep on a chopstick, and it left a deep mark on my face that wouldn't fade. I studied it in the mirror. I pressed it. There was no pain. Then I pulled back my hair and descended to the street. I bought my coffee at the cart. The vendor paused. The glass globe of the pot was suspended in his hand. He pointed at my face. What happened? I studied my reflection in the window of the pastry case, behind which lay rows of buns and rolls. The bruise extended to my temple and was of a dark purple color that carried the echo of abuse. I shrugged. I slept funny, I said. He looked at me an extra beat. Poured. On the house, he said.

At work, other women lingered in the break room. I walked by them with my bruise. I sharpened a pencil and sat down at my desk. I set a page into my typewriter and wrote, *This image*. I paused, trying to think of what to say other than *is salable*. I felt like walking upstairs and asking you directly, What is this bruise I have? Instead I ran through the list of objects I was supposed to be describing, portraits of Surrealist painters with their pets. Muralists emerged from the Parisian Métro with anteaters on leashes. They posed with ocelots. The pet was a muse, the inspiration, or so I was supposed to say. Only I couldn't. Constance had told me these photographs were brilliant. What did she see in them that I could not? I wondered who would ever pay so much for a photo of Magritte's dog. I pushed myself from the desk and went down the hall to ask my boss.

I would have rather been working on the collection of pastels Constance had been assigned. They weren't even for sale. I loved the bathers, French prostitutes stepping in and out of claw-footed tubs, thick flanks streaked with green. I went to visit them after work. The bathers always kept a date, and I loved them for that. They went away on loan and came back soon. It was my mother who'd told me Impressionists collected shades of green. They kept lists. Emeralds. Teal. The lime of a sun-stricken leaf. The whole world was slightly green.

I stopped at the door and knocked, twisted my hands in the fabric of my clothes. My boss was on the phone. It's an investment, she was saying. It's of a piece with its time. It *is* time, she said, and in that statement I could hear the echo of the wall text I had written, the sort of declaration that failed me now. And why? That's all I had come to discuss. My boss fiddled with the spiral phone cord. Can you hold? She hushed the receiver and looked at me, waiting for me to speak. I felt very aware of my appearance in that moment. The arrangement of my body. The bruise on my face. My hair was falling from its knob, pins slipping, and my chest failed to fill the front of the dress. The bruise was a shadow, a deep and muddy purple, and could easily have been mistaken for a streak of dirt. I felt her look at me in the same way I had just been looking at those pictures: unsure what to make of the image in front of her. I wanted to ask, would it be possible for me to work anywhere but in this building, where you were just upstairs? I thought of the actress from Mme Popov's. After auditions, she paced the apartment, complaining at the top of her lungs, silk ribbons to her kimono flying. Once someone yelled back from the street, *Keep trying, baby!* and she flung open the window and leaned over the sill to reply, *What the fuck else do you think I'm trying to do?* My boss sat in silence, still muffling the receiver. And before I could stop myself, before I was able to recall that I was no actress, really, I had no other parts to audition for, I told her I would like to quit. Just a second, she said, then put the buyer back on hold. I stood in the door in my too-large dress. I thought my boss might try to dissuade me, she would make a case for me to stay. I hoped she would. I had done so well, I was precocious, I should return to my desk. But what she said was, Are you sure? I tilted on my borrowed heels. Yes. She nodded. Good luck to you, she said.

Later, at home, I sat in the window with a plate of toast and watched debris gather in the air shaft. Really, I said out loud to the room. I think it's for the best.

THREE

I

How far away my fiancé seemed! He was all the way on the other side of the room. It might have been a mile. But I suppose I've never been one for keeping track of distances or time. Minutes, hours, the whole of my youth: I looked up and saw that they had gone. I was still crouched on the doormat, and my limbs were radios out of range, full of static, asleep. I lowered my forehead to my knees as a fresh spell of nausea constricted my throat.

There is something about feeling ill that has always made me especially formal and polite. On the subway, in the moment before I sense I am about to faint, I become a perfect lady. I'm sorry, I hate to bother you. So sorry, excuse me, but I believe I need to sit down. Now I brought my palms to my cheeks and felt they were damp with sweat. The apartment dilated, and within that exaggerated scope I could sense some locus of concern. Perhaps it belonged to my fiancé. I gathered the skirts of my traveling dress. Pardon me, I said. The floor acquired a certain tilt, and I took this opportunity to pitch toward the bath, where I knelt on the tiles that had always been such a pain to clean, I remembered, back when I was responsible for cleaning them. I shifted my knees. Locked the door. This is a reason to marry, I thought. To have someone always at your side when you are about to retch.

It is a strange feeling, to be shut in a bathroom that once belonged to you. I washed my face. The faucet struck the same shrill notes it always had, and thin streetlight filtered through the narrow window. I looked around. There was the porcelain sink. The tub. Peering behind the curtain, I found an unfamiliar brand of soap.

I stood at the sink, water dripping down my nose and onto the dress. My reflection hovered in the mirror. I was pale. I opened the flimsy door of the medicine cabinet and looked in at the toothpaste, mouthwash, the little spools of floss, a single bottle of perfume. I lifted it, spritzed. The rest of the apartment was conspicuously absent any sign of woman. And yet here she was. She had a whole shelf of her own. I recalled retreating to my parents' bedroom as a girl to search through the drawers that still held my mother's things. The woman my fiancé was seeing now had similar tastes. Lipstick, blush, nail files of various lengths and grains. No eye makeup, as far as I could tell. I touched the pink handle of a razor. A vial of varnish capped in gold. In the wilderness of a boar's brush alighted a bramble of hair a few shades lighter than my own. I selected the lipstick, unwound a fresh inch of maroon, brought it partway to my lips. Then I looked in the mirror. I silently recapped the tube, replaced everything just as it had been.

A lot of life, maybe, rests on a profound misremembering. On the substitution of the familiar for the strange. It is all too tempting to look for meaningful connections, signs of fate, when most relationships amount to no more than a terrible coincidence, a grand confusion of crimson paints. Perhaps my fiancé was right: the link between Persephone Q and me was no stronger than the bonds I formed with contemporaneous browsers on America Online, in the annals of the Shopping page. Those exchanges of proximity and contingency so easily mistaken for direct address. I thought they were speaking to me! But of course they don't think twice about you, these other users, they click away and never know you at all. The idea made me feel sick once more, and also very tired. I thought of the Russian in the Met. The sadness in his eyes.

I emerged from the bath plain and damp. My fiancé was still seated on the bed, staring at some invisible point of interest on the floor. Maybe he was remembering. Certainly I was remembering. Only, it seemed we were remembering different things. The rug undulated blue. Seasick, I made my way to the sofa and lay down. The ceiling pressed in like the prow of an incoming ship. There was Persephone, the figurehead. I closed my eyes. I recalled how victorious it used to feel to be out in the city with my fiancé. I was too admiring, too prone to starstruck states. But you can't admire everything, not everything can be a surprise. That's the thing, with taste. Eventually you have to choose. I looked down the length of the sofa at my bare and calloused feet.

Are you all right?

My fiancé was standing before the bed, still holding his keys.

Only pregnant, I said.

Congratulations.

You don't think it's a good idea, do you?

I never said that.

I plan on being an excellent mother.

I'm sure you will be, he said.

———

I missed Misha. Also Brahms. There must be some way to find a joke in all this, I thought, and together they would know how. I glanced at the clock. There was half an hour until Misha was due to give his presentation. Just enough time, if I rushed. I ought to call a cab. Instead I shivered, turned onto my side. As soon as I was sure that I could stand, I'd go.

Tell me, did you send that package?

What package?

I looked at him.

Never mind.

My fiancé disappeared from view. I heard the faucet singing in the sink. Then he reappeared with a glass of water. Here, he said. I took a cautious sip, handed it back to him. He hovered, glass half full. I felt a strange sense of déjà vu. He must have felt it, too. Just then he stepped away. He glanced at the poster overhead.

You're really sure it's you?

My body stretched before me on the sofa.

I said, I know how we can check.

◈

I never did discover where my mother went that night she took the car out on her own. We asked around. We had to ask around. It had to do with how you price a death, because not all deaths are worth the same. For a long time I imagined she had a lover, or a friend, people she visited whom my father and I had never met. These fragile affiliations grew elaborately, like daisy chains, in my child mind. Now I often wonder if she simply drove to the city to walk the streets alone at night, see the things she liked to see. I doubt she ever meant to leave us so permanently. I liked to imagine her, sometimes, weaving through the same blocks that I frequented from day to day. She was there in the Garment District, watching her reflection leap between the windows, admiring the glitter of the sequins on display. She sat on a bench by the Egyptian obelisk, behind the Met, and wondered, as I have from time to time, How many of these monuments were uprooted from the deserts, and how many still remain? She was there in the laundromat, converting dollars into coins. This was the upside to not knowing enough. I could imagine her however I pleased. I wondered if I'd recognize her, were I to see her now. If, in my visions of her, she'd recognize herself.

I was still unstable as I followed my fiancé up the ladder and to the atelier. My hands shook. My face was damp. I wore my pink trench, hat, scarf, prepared to dash. I checked my pockets for cash and keys while he sat at his desk.

You'll be quick?

My fiancé nodded.

It's easy, he said.

The monitor illuminated. He tapped a password into the dialog box. The skylight was a black square in the ceiling, and beneath it, where we used to keep our bed, a space had been cleared to accommodate a reflector screen and a small wooden portrait chair. I peeked over the edge of the loft, into the living room. Then I returned to my fiancé's shoulder to watch the hourglass slowly spin.

Oh, come on, he said.

One thing I had not told my fiancé was how long I had lain there on the bed that morning after the shutter snapped. The flash lingered in the room. I was pinioned, maybe, by a sense of premonition. But I've always lived my life too slow. As a girl, after departing from the upper stories of the tree in our front yard, I could sense that something serious in me had shifted, and yet I was not sufficiently alarmed. The branches hashed the blue sky overhead. How many hours passed, I wonder, before two arms came to scoop me up from the snow and carry me to the car?

On-screen, the hourglass yielded. He entered commands, navigating fluidly. Windows opened onto further windows until an image of Persephone Q appeared. The room was furnished. The skyline, complete. It was the original image from the show, the one on which all the other, emptier versions were based. Though I was wary of making assumptions. I thought by now I'd have been desensitized to the sight of myself, catatonic on the bed. Standing so close to the man who'd captured it, however, I saw it fresh. It was a portrait of stubborn slumber. Only those with too much trust are able to sleep that way.

I pointed at my rib cage.

The scar is here, I said.

My fiancé nodded. Then he set to work. He partitioned the image the way you lay claim to a piece of land. The selected area drew near. The surrounding room, the walls, the furniture, the skyline were pushed from view. He staked another claim, cropped my ribs, tapped a key.

We drew nearer still. A drop-down menu appeared, and he navigated it, manipulated the pixels-per-parts, the digital thread count. The image sharpened. My body was becoming a pale, abstract thing: a shape, a color swatch. We were far too close for comfort. You need to be at some distance, I think, to appreciate humanity. Perhaps that's what all the trouble is. We do our gazing far too close, or else too far away. Like Rothkos. No one ever looks at them correctly. The artist thought the ideal distance from which to view his six-foot swaths of color was six inches. He wanted you to stand right there with the canvas against your nose. You can't see anything that close. The whole composition dissolves. So it was with Persephone. We zoomed. A bit of texture appeared beneath an arm. Is that it? my fiancé asked. He refined the image again. The quality was poor and pixelated, a block of scaled skin. It looked less like me than ever. I don't know, I said. I reached. The screen met my fingertip convexly, delivered a shock of static. And the doorbell rang.

Few sounds were more upsetting than the motor of that buzzer. It ground into our thoughts. My fiancé checked his watch once more. After another moment, he pushed himself from the desk, descended the ladder. He paused for a moment at the door, staring at his shoes. Then disappeared into the hall.

2

Alone, I looked at the screen. At the abstruse beauty of what may or may not have been a scar. Then I crossed the atelier and collapsed into the portrait chair. The poster of Persephone Q hung before me in the rafters. I sat. Very still. Having a staring contest with myself. I was really sick of her.

It strikes me there are fewer private moments now. There is a great race on, really. The goal is to gather your own impressions before someone else can tell you what you saw, what you are seeing. To be the consumer rather than the consumed. Information proliferates not in pursuit of the new but according to the law of averages: extremes converge, and we hover dumbly around the mean. I find myself more and more sympathetic, of late, to adventurers, tornado chasers, collectors of orchids and exotic fish. I look them up online. I suppose they are only in search of something of their own, for the chance to be alone, arrest the subtle slippage of the self that occurs whenever other people are around. I stood to go. Downstairs, a door crashed distantly. Two sets of footsteps sounded on the steps, voices in the vestibule. I buttoned my coat. It would be the owner of the lipstick in the medicine cabinet, maybe, and I was hardly eager for us to meet. I wished her well. Then the door opened, and my fiancé appeared. I paused. There, behind him, I was astonished to find not the woman I'd extrapolated from the razor and the lipstick, a deep maroon, but Misha. He looked only slightly less surprised to see me.

Percy, he said. What are you doing up there?

For a brief moment before that buzzer sounded, I had enjoyed a spell of resolution. Maybe it wasn't me in the picture. Maybe it was, if only in my mind. And what was the difference, really, between empirical evidence and personal belief? I was convinced. Now that Misha had arrived, however, empiricism quickly regained the upper hand. It was empirically bad that I was here, in my fiancé's loft, rather than at the expo center, where I'd said I'd be. It was empirically bad that a large nude photograph of my person hung overhead, visible to both my former and my current lovers, deleterious indeed that in order to exit the loft I had to turn my back on these men and slowly make my way down the ladder, thus presenting my ass, which was not, empirically, my most attractive feature. It was a disaster all around. There was nothing to say. I descended slowly, carefully, too resigned to rush. My whole body seemed disposable, a little tuft of tissue tucked around a gift. I reached the floor quite sick, certain that Misha had come to dispose of me.

Outside, it was dark. A silence passed. Everyone was waiting for me to speak. I was the reason we were here, after all. I wanted to say, Let's all go home. But it was rather too late to retreat. My fiancé took pity on me. So, he said. I guess you two know each other? He offered tea, whiskey, wine, as if it were the most natural thing in the world for him to be hosting us. I wanted to leave that instant and was about to explain we couldn't stay. Misha slipped off his coat.

I'll take vodka.

Right, my fiancé said. Vodka it is.

He turned to the kitchenette.

I looked at my husband. He was dressed for his presentation. Tweed jacket and jeans, the shoes, as we'd discussed. A stack of poster boards was pinned beneath his arm. He set it down. The contents of my totes were still scattered across the floor, and it struck me that this was as good a time as any to gather them. I knelt, chasing lip balms and pens, legal precedents. Misha stooped and selected one of the images I'd sliced from the exhibition book. In this particular iteration, the red room was especially empty, and I seemed especially exposed. Misha held it to the light.

I've had an interesting call from a reporter. It seems that this is you?

I sighed.

I guess that's a matter of debate.

Misha folded the photograph into his pocket. Then he crossed the room and sat on the sofa, directly below the poster of Persephone. I sat beside him, running my palms along the embossed velvet of the upholstery, up and down, up and down, until he placed his hands on mine to bring them to a halt.

How did you know where I was?

Misha shrugged.

It's the only pink house on the street.

I frowned.

I didn't know I told you that.

My fiancé emerged from the kitchenette, bottle of vodka wedged under his arm. Three glasses chimed on the table. He poured a shot into each and placed one before me—conspicuously, I thought. I watched Misha tip his back in a single swallow. Then he poured another. And another. Misha often enjoyed a vodka or two, or three.

At home, his chess set doubled as a fleet of vials: the king's crown was a hinge. Why not? I myself had drunk the volume of a fallen bishop. I always lost when we played chess, I couldn't keep up, and Misha drank the contents of my captured pieces for me. He held his liquor better than anyone I knew. However, discovering your wife clinging to a ladder in her ex-fiancé's loft will leave even the strongest liver compromised. He should slow down. Misha, I said. I was about to tell him to stop. Then he downed my vodka, too, and energetically began to pace the room.

Pacing was a hobby of Misha's. He used to study this way, crossing the bedroom back and forth with a textbook balanced in his palms. When he reached a challenging passage he paused to run a finger down the page. He went to the river to think. In my fiancé's apartment, the ceiling sloped so low that Misha had to stoop as he traversed the room. The windows caught flashes of his reflection as he passed, caches for a rapidly moving data set. Outside, through the rain, the skyline had emerged. How many more months, I wondered, until I was no longer shocked whenever I looked south? Ground level, the city stirred. Anticipation drifted up from the streets. People were going for drinks, for dinner, to functions like the one to which Misha should have already arrived, and which he very much needed to attend. The whole event was beginning now. Instead, he paced my fiancé's floors. I watched his sharp shoulders, thin face, his wrists and legs, the small belly nestled beneath the high button of his jacket. He was so pale the light seemed to sink into him an inch, it filtered through him like one of Claire's figurines, illuminating subcutaneous layers of being. And currently that core flushed red. I had seen Misha this agitated only once before, and that was when the Patriot Act was passed. There was nothing patriotic about it, he said. The public's obsession with tapping phones only distracted from the far greater danger of legalizing cyber spies. The only thing worse, he felt, than sharing your name, email, browsing history, library records, and IP address with a corporation like Insta-Ad was to cede it to the government instead. It was the Iron Curtain all over again. He was just as worked up now, as he addressed my fiancé:

So let me get this straight. You took a picture without permission. And then decided—still without permission—to turn it into a show. You do not tell my wife. But neither do you, Misha said, turning to me. You don't tell me anything. You go to Claire and reporters and galleries. And so I am standing around like an idiot. I have to wait for someone to call me at work to find out that anything is going on.

He mimed answering the phone.

"Oh, hi, do you believe your wife?" Again like an idiot I am saying, "Who is this?" and "Sure I do." "Oh, okay," she says. "How is this affecting your relationship at home?" As if I'd say anything so personal over the phone! But of course the answer is not so good. It isn't affecting my relationship well. I am telling you all the time not to give out our information. This is why.

At some point during this speech, Misha had managed to slip his thin arms into his overcoat. The hem of it flapped around his ankles as he paced, substantiating speed. He strode across the carpet to the stack of poster boards, tucked them under his arm.

Misha, I said.

Is there something else you would like to tell me, or do I have it right?

I was silent.

Good. Then I am set.

He stepped onto the landing. The door closed with a click.

I stood for a moment in the center of the room. I could hear Misha's beleaguered progress as he maneuvered an entire presentation down the stairs. Then I hurried. I took my purse by its strap, lifted my totes. Leaving proved no easier than arriving; stacks of *Am J Tra Las* eased from the canvas and onto the floor. I turned to my fiancé. Keep them, I said.

At the door, I paused. My fiancé was again sitting on the bed, as he had when I presented to him the other exhibition, the one that couldn't be viewed. I couldn't decide what feeling it was I harbored for him. I pitied him, I suppose, for being just as inept as I was, in life and in love. Well, it was nice to see you, he said. He looked into the kitchen, through the wall, toward the street. You probably should have told him, he added. I nodded. I wrapped my arms around my totes. It seemed I'd arrived years ago. I took one last look at the apartment, rested a hand on the knob of the door. Look, I said. If anyone asks, can you just tell them the truth? My fiancé turned an empty shot glass in his hands. Of course, he said. I'll try.

Perhaps you never know you love something until it is under threat. Outside, I stood in the drizzle, looking up and down the block with a sense of mild terror. Then I saw Misha lumbering to the corner, encumbered by poster boards and printouts of his slides. I easily caught up. Here, I said. Let me help. I siphoned off a cardboard triptych and slipped it under my arm. It was the size of a man, and progress was even slower with my totes. We passed through the narrow chamber of a stretch of scaffolding. The green supports rose to either side, like trees. The drizzle turned to rain, and there was no more snow. I tucked my chin into my collar as other couples hurried past. Heels clacked on wet cement. Arms wrapped around shoulders as beautiful people disappeared into foyers, doorways, bars. Posters pinned, Misha and I moved like penguins to the corner, where he raised his free arm and hailed a cab. He opened the door, tossed the sodden presentation into the back. I ran around to the other side and slid into the opposite seat before he could drive off. The cabbie glanced into the rearview mirror. Where do you want to go? Misha mumbled the address. Then he directed his gaze out the window, away from me. The car set off with a splash.

We rode in silence, trapped in our thoughts. The driver must have intuited something had come between us. *Can't you see they're breaking up?* He shuttered the plastic divider separating the seats. I wished he'd turn the radio on. Then I wouldn't have to think at all. Outside, people huddled beneath umbrellas, collapsed umbrellas into spires, righted spokes turned inside out. There were always people caught without cover in the rain, and yet, it seemed to me, enough umbrellas to go around. The cabs glistened like persimmons. Shoppers mulled under awnings and in doorways, sprinted across the street, eliciting horns. Misha gathered the handles to my totes and pulled the weight of them across the seats. We looked into the jumble of tea and tampons and books and knives.

Let me take these, he said.

It's fine.

The rule of thumb is don't lift more than twenty pounds.

I glanced at him, confused.

When pregnant, that is.

I sighed.

Oh, Misha. How did you know?

He shrugged.

I found the test in the trash weeks ago.

I folded my hands over the rise of my belly. What a fool I was. Misha had known all along. It was worse than discovering old pictures of yourself. He'd broken the fourth wall of my own charade.

I meant to tell you so many times, I said. Then there was this package, the exhibition—

The cab halted abruptly as a woman dashed across the street.

No one believed me, I said.

Warehouses loomed at the end of the block. The taxi crawled between luxury buildings with Hudson views. Traffic accumulated at the entrance to the highway, and we came to a halt. Our voices were loud without the rush of the car. Misha looked at his hands.

Do you like being married to me?

Of course I do.

Really?

Yes, how can you ask?

Then why don't you tell me anything and never come to bed?

I propped my elbows on my knees, my head in my palms. I was forgetting what it was like not to feel nauseated all the time.

What if I told you it's because I accidentally tried to kill you? And not just once.

Misha frowned.

Are you sure?

The car lurched forward, and we jostled back. Misha's profile was bleak in the window. I noticed how his cheeks had sharpened, the usual hollows burrowing deeper between the bones. His cowlick had grown severe. How much we'd changed, I thought, in no time at all. I'd loved Misha completely before the package arrived, before I pinched his nose. And yet I felt I loved him much more now. It was impossible, illogical, for both to be true at once. He released his seat belt as we drew into the lot.

You should probably ask Yvette about that hand.

I looked at the bandage, where the tape was coming loose.

I already did, I said.

———

In front of the expo center, men milled about in suits. Misha straightened his tweed jacket, smoothed his jeans. He gathered his posters, my totes. Together we stood on the curb, beneath the banner. *TechHype 2001!* Let me help, I said. I wanted to be there to hear him give his talk. Misha hitched the totes on his shoulders and the poster boards under his arm, shook his head. I started to follow, and he held up his hand. I am sorry, he said. I can't think with you around.

He disappeared through the mouth of the warehouse like another consumer good. I watched him go. I admired Misha very much for his work, his view of the world. For the very fact that he had somewhere to be, while I did not. The cab pulled away in a spray of rain and oil. Alone, I turned up the street. I felt decidedly vulnerable, unsubstantiated, stripped of all my totes.

3

It's funny now to think how easily I might have missed my own exhibition. I might not have opened that package, might not have received any mail at all. The glass of the door had been shattered, and someone else could have reached through the gap. Upon tearing away the tape, maybe she, too, would have seen herself in that series of photographs. I had been so certain, when I returned to the pink house, that I was Persephone Q. Now I no longer knew what to believe. I wondered what the sender of the package had meant for me to see.

I caught an uptown train to City College, roamed the empty streets. I felt sick of my old haunts, my block, the laundromat. I was tired of being alone. I took to Broadway, where the vegetable stands were closed. No bicycles spun in the street, though the rain had eased. I veered east and sat for a while on a wet swing set, looking out onto Hamilton's house, until the soft swaying coaxed forth the urge to be sick. How much history should we preserve? I thought. Just enough to make it seem that not much has been lost. I walked on, calculating the hours until Misha came home. He would not even have begun his talk by this time. Then would come all the presentations after his, the drinks and networking, the exchanging of business cards, all the little ceremonies I ought to be there for. I sighed. A rat darted out of a trash can, another on its tail. I stepped aside. I abandoned the playground for quiet, brownstoned blocks. The storefront churches were asleep, corrugated tin drawn over their mouths. Black plastic bundles piled high along the curbs. A flyer fluttered by and I fixed it flat against the pavement with my sneaker: it was an invitation to a block party, dated yesterday.

I turned back toward the playground, spied into lit apartments lined with books. At the intersection, I caught sight of a dim red glow. My heart leapt a little. My psychic was in! I hadn't seen her in what felt like months but could have only been a week. I hurried one block south.

My psychic kept irregular and impulsive hours. It was impossible to plan. I often had better luck walking by her storefront lair in the very early morning or late at night on a whim, rather than arriving during the hours listed on her door.

I stood outside. The neon sign seared its advertisement onto the night: TAROT READINGS. I buzzed. An anthropomorphic moon and sun occupied the awning, surrounded by a smattering of stars. The lock released, and I pushed through. The plush curtains were drawn over the windows and along the walls, blocking out the light and absorbing all the sound. It was a sensory vacuum, that velvet room. The street, the swing set, Hamilton's house could have been miles away. Who knew what time it was? All sense of time was moot. The scalloped patterns on the carpet fluttered across the floor to where my psychic was sitting on a pouf, knitting. I stood in the entrance and watched her loop new yarn onto the needle. Knit, purl. Knit, purl. The garment growing into her lap had the shape of a mitten, or maybe a hat. Either way, I was not about to interrupt. I watched her knit another row. Then she carefully counted her stitches and set her work aside. Percy, she said. I knew you'd be back.

I slid into a folding chair. Crystals swung from my psychic's neck as she set the kettle on the hot plate, clusters of pendants that glinted violet and sand and gray. Her hair was gathered high and pinned in place, and in the low lamplight it shone not unlike a crown. My psychic was the most imperious woman I knew, I decided. Not even the self-help author could compete. As the water boiled, she slid the knitting needles through her hair. A stack of tarot cards appeared from the pocket of an apron wrapped snugly around her waist. Percy, she said. You're a diamond in the rough. How can I help? She held out her hands and I gave her my wrists. Her thumbs were cool on my veins. Tense, she said. I can feel it. Your blood is taut. She took up the deck and shuffled it into three separate stacks, flipped the top cards with a knowing hum. The Empress. The Hermit. The Seven of Cups. My psychic pressed. What's on your mind? I watched the kettle shiver on the plate. Remember, I said, a little while ago, when you said I had those spirits in me? She nodded. They're in you still, she said. She closed her eyes, waded through the energies in the room. Even more now than there were before? I asked. Yes, I think that's right. The neon sign crackled behind the curtains, blinking on and off. The office was open, closed, open, closed, even as I sat inside. I smoothed the wool of my traveling dress. I'm pregnant, I said. The psychic smiled, tapped a card. That explains the Empress, she replied. Though I sat very still in the folding chair, I could feel something in me respond. The nebula seemed to quiver. For the first time I felt I could register its presence, nascent. My psychic reached for another card. I watched her slow, deliberate hands. It occurred to me that she was only repeating everything I said. I was telling her the truth of me, rather than the other way around. This was no use. I wanted to rid myself of whatever it was, resident in me, that had pushed Misha and those I loved aside. I didn't want to disappear from Morningside. But the others, I said. Can't you just . . . evict them? My psychic laughed, then sadly shook her head. It doesn't work like that, she said. She revealed the Magician. The Lovers, reversed. The Five of Cups. I no longer wished to know my fate or have my fortune told. I reached into my pocket for crumpled cash. My hand met the dog-eared photograph. I'll pay you back, I promise, I said. But right now I have to go.

There aren't so many comforts in this life. Maybe that's how you know that you are growing old. You burn through solace more quickly than before, though conservation is the required mode. It used to be enough to sprawl on the carpet while my mother vacuumed around my limbs, accept protective charms, clip coupons with Yvette's mother as she nursed a cigarette—in my mind's eye I watched the orange tip of her menthol recede into the past. I felt an acute sense of finitude. The profundity of all I lacked. There was no one left to plug me in so that my world lit up like a neon sign. I put a hand to my belly, where the nebula buzzed. From now on it might be just you and me, I thought.

It would be at least another hour until Misha came home. If he did come home. I imagined the two of us in summer, on East Tenth, walking arm in arm to the tune of Hungarian Dance. How far away that seemed. The avenue before me was deserted, abandoned to the dark and the mist that brews after rain. I walked the length of Morningside Park. The landscape rose out of the shadows, presenting luminous boulders, the flat of the pond. I ducked into a bodega for a jar of olives. Who could explain these cravings? They came to me, and I obeyed. Back on the damp paths of the park, I braced the jar against a knee and wrestled with the lid. The safety seal would not budge. I tried again. In my fiancé's exhibition I had seemed so powerfully serene. I was a veritable symbol, a woman immune to the passage of time. What a mythic force she was, that woman on the bed. And why is it always a woman, I wondered, who knows all but stands aside, indifferent as the Fates? I thought of my mother. I wrestled the jar. Perhaps I should have aspired to a life of more

Homeric proportions. As things stood, it was nine o'clock, and I was on the street, in the mist, at war with a condiment.

The night was ornate with after-rain. Lampposts glistened. The lights of the college rolled through the trees, down the hill, diffused over the grass and ragged outcrops of snow. I looked down the length of the lawn, to the point where the avenue kinks and splits, and the old apartment buildings stand ornery and overwrought. Someone was walking north beneath the canopy of elms. He wasn't moving very fast. Jar in hand, I set off at a clip. This was my hero. A knight sent to open the jar. Then his gait grew familiar as I neared. He seemed to sway. I wondered, could it really be? I recalled my trek to the laundromat with the self-help author to see if it was Harold she'd spotted at the dryers. For a moment I was afraid. He couldn't be back. And if he was—what an apology he owed! As did we. We hadn't believed Claire, we'd called her insane, and she had been right all along. No matter how kind Harold had been to me—moving furniture, loaning blenders, granting entry whenever I forgot my keys—he'd rather put Claire through hell. Only to return, as she knew he would. But that's how it goes. It isn't so simple to disappear, I was learning. In fact, nothing goes. Everything resurfaces in time. I was mentally drafting a self-righteous manifesto along these lines when the figure entered a pool of lamplight. The face that appeared was extremely recognizable. It wasn't Harold's at all.

◈

Each time I saw Buck, I had to relearn not to stare. After a poetry reading, he lingered in my thoughts. I worried about him. Then I forgot. The sore on his nose slipped my mind until I ran into him like this on the street, or at the diner, where he went daily for a slice of quiche, newspaper tucked under his arm. The cashier greeted him: The same? It was always the same. I wondered if Buck returned so often because that way people never forgot, or else they grew so used to him they no longer had a reason to stare. I stood on the sidewalk now, determined not to gawk.

The sore glimmered faintly, like an oil spill. I focused on his clothes. Buck's pants were cinched high around a very thin waist, revealing anemic, opalescent ankles, his skin stretched tightly around the bone. The temperature had dropped and his overcoat struck me as too thin. The wool fell loosely over his arms and failed to cover his pale wrists. He stared at me with an intensity I found difficult to bear.

I held up the jar.

I was just trying to open these olives, I said.

We watched the green fruits bobbing in the marinade, the pimientos flashing orange. I asked Buck where he was off to, what he was doing out on this dreary night. He'd gotten a late start on his trip to the diner that day. In fact, he was on his way now. He tapped his cane on the sidewalk and turned to me. Did I care to join? Oh, Buck, I said. He nearly broke my heart with his old-fashioned ideas about how to treat a woman you meet on the street: of course you ask her along. TVs flared blue in windows. Across the avenue, a kitchen bloomed with light. I watched a silhouette empty a bowl. I was unsure what to do about Buck, and also reluctant to leave. Here he was, in the cold, poking his nose into exactly those conditions it ought to avoid. I thought of bringing him to the self-help author's, but that would mean going home. I wasn't ready to face the apartment on my own.

Hey, I said. You know who has good quiche?

Buck shrugged.

I'll take you, if you're up for a walk.

He was. I led the way across the street.

On the trek across town to the bus, I stared at my sneakers and the sidewalk and the street. For a moment or two, I'd forget about Buck's sore. Then I'd look up and there it'd be, passionately purple in the light of a chicken joint. I looked away. It put the exhibition, my marriage, my olive jar into rather harsh perspective, that sore.

Many blocks went by in silence. I wished I could have called upon the self-help author for help. She always knew just what to say. Near the top of the park, people spilled in and out of restaurants and bars and supermarkets, filling the streets. Buck and I sat on a bench at the bus stop by the minty glow of a toothpaste ad. When the M4 arrived, I dipped my card twice. Buck took a handicap seat in the front, and I sat directly across. I announced, to no one in particular: I'm expecting, you know. The bus stopped and started around the north end of the park, turned down Museum Mile. Out the window, on the slick and gleaming street, the monoliths passed in granite bursts. Banners unfurled across the entrances, announcing exhibitions. *American Quilts and Textile Arts*. I wondered if Misha might like to go. The man next to me was filling in the crossword, and I watched him complete four empty squares. D-O-J-O. He erased, thought, traced the letters again. Buck's chin fell to his chest. When our stop arrived, I tugged gently at his sleeve. Almost there, I said. He reached for his cane, still half in a dream.

We left the bright of the bus for the dark of the night. On the street, Buck raised his eyes, no longer afraid to meet anyone's gaze. We passed the hotels, wine bars, brassy shops wholly devoted to one accessory apiece: bags, shoes, watches. Diners spun pasta onto forks. Buck cupped his hand at the window of a basement bar. An elderly gentleman looked up from a plate of crab claws, startled. Hey, I said. Just a few more blocks.

The streets grew emptier, the brownstones solemn and serene. Then came the high-rises, the medical offices: the hospital rose before us like a theater in its flash of lights. I hadn't told Buck where we were going. Now the complex made a great roadblock against the river and the sky. He froze, refusing to take another step. I tried to be matter-of-fact. They have fantastic food, I said. His wound was ruby and frantic in the glow of a passing ambulance. A whole fleet of emergency vehicles passed as I cajoled him in the dark. We were too close, I reasoned, for him to turn back. Please, I said. Recalling the self-help author's words about the power of touch, I placed a palm on his arm. Buck jerked away in reflexive disgust. I promise, I said. I have a friend who works here. I come all the time, just to eat. He scowled, face twisting around his sore. With despair he looked back down the long blocks we had walked. Finally, he agreed.

4

Hospitals are one of the few places you can trust never to close. Emergency rooms, subways, laundromats: they keep the old adage alive. Buck and I moved through the sliding doors, past the security guards. The slippery lobby was dotted with tented yellow caution signs, and doctors darted between. The marble floors met glass walls overlooking stony gardens. The coffee shop was closed, the grate drawn and locked. I watched a custodian wheel a tub of trash into an elevator. I turned to Buck. This way, I said.

The cafeteria was deserted. Visiting hours were nearly over, and attendants were clearing the buffet. I took two trays and gave one to Buck. What ensued was a feast. We loaded casseroles, sandwiches, little pastries on paper plates. To my great relief, there really was quiche, and I was glad to see I hadn't lied. I recited Yvette's account number from memory, then wandered through the empty rows of tables to a remote seat. Hunched on low stools, we silently devoured trays of Hamburger Helper, dinner rolls, and spinach, creamed, washed it down with coffee dispensed hot and black and automatic from the machine. Buck ate two slices of quiche Lorraine, and I had a slice myself. As we sank into dessert, the last of the visitors wandered through the aisles, looking for the exit, for popsicles, for juice. A small boy in pajamas stared at Buck with open wonder. He tugged his mother's arm. She glanced at us, then hurried along.

Shh, she said. It isn't nice to stare.

Departing whispers echoed on the linoleum. Cookware clanged distantly in an industrial sink. Our table was a plundered village of crumpled napkins and soiled plates. Buck peeled the foil from a thimble of cream and tipped it into his cup. I felt my eyes droop. The cafeteria was soporific, the air thickly layered with the salty scent of food. I felt I could lie across it, as in the Dead Sea, and go straight to sleep. I lowered my lids. When I looked up again, Buck was staring at my unfinished slice of chocolate cake. I pushed it across the table toward him, then rested my chin in my hands and watched him eat. Across the room, reflected in the opaque window glass, Buck's face was vague and dignified, but when I turned back to the man as he was, the reality of the rot could not be denied. He ran the edge of his fork around the saucer, scooping crumbs. Buck, I said. Have you really seen someone about your nose? His face shuttered, like a house in a storm. He sank his fork into a cold mound of macaroni and brought his shoulders toward his tray. I lowered my chin so that we were eye to eye. Have you? He mumbled. He was afraid, he said, that there was nothing the doctors could do. I nodded. Maybe, I said. But would knowing that leave you any worse off than you are now?

At the buffet, a cafeteria worker appeared and began loading Styrofoam saucers of cake into a tub. Buck watched him longingly.

I went across the room and took another slice. He ate delicately, saving the frieze of frosting for last. Then he folded a napkin and dabbed carefully at his lips, so as not to dab his wound. His face was a grandfather clock, wide and open with a dark torque at the center, wound to the hour of neglect.

I hate hospitals, he said.

We passed the ER, the main entrance, arrived at the visitors' desk, where I told the woman at the reception that I was here to see a friend. She looked at me skeptically, glanced at my thumb. I was tired of these receptionists. It was as if they'd banded together to blacklist me from the use of public space. I gave her Yvette's name. Ring her up, I said. Send a page. The receptionist made her calls. Then—and all too reluctantly, I thought—a machine printed out two passes of hunting-season-orange. Place it here, I said to Buck, peeling away the sticker-back to one and securing the badge to my breast. He did the same. The neon competed for attention with the ravage of his face.

At the elevator bank, staggered lights blinked on and off in simple patterns, illuminating progress on floors above. The carriage slid open, and we got in. It was a Shabbat elevator out of order, because though it was not Saturday, it stopped on every floor before finally depositing us onto Yvette's ward. Buck tucked his chin into the collar of his coat, suddenly self-conscious. The halls were tracked with fluorescent lights. Red alarms blinked above recovery rooms, where soap opera scores mingled with the chirping of equipment. Buck and I pressed flat against the wall to let a stretcher pass. I punched a button and two glass doors sighed open royally, leading to post-op, where patients walked prescribed laps around the halls, trailing dollies. Buck and I joined, caboose to the moribund procession. Then we found Yvette. She was at the nurses' station, delivering instructions at the change of shift. Her hands were lost in the pockets of her scrubs and her eyes were rimmed with red. She saw us and stuttered. I motioned to Buck, who'd fallen behind, shuffling his uneven steps and leaning on his cane. After the briefest hesitation, Yvette set her shock aside. Her face was blank. I tried to make mine the same. I said, We have a favor to ask. Yvette held up a hand. She didn't want to know. It was better to schedule the surgery first, then ask what insurance he had.

◈

So much red tape keeps people apart. I waited with Buck on the ward to receive the paperwork. I was prepared to wait until morning. I wasn't sure if Misha would return, and I still couldn't stand to face the vacant bed. Then a social worker came by, administering rules and regulations. She notched the clipboard in her elbow.

I'm afraid you'll need to go.

I looked at Buck, then back to her.

Are you sure?

Are you family?

I shook my head.

You should have been gone hours ago.

I gathered my coat. From the nearest room, I could hear the steady sighs of a breathing machine. I said to Buck, I'll see you soon. Then I walked slowly toward the automatic doors. The social worker's questions followed me down the hall. *Occupation? Any family at all? Current place of residence?* I turned. She was imposing in the fluorescent lights, pen poised. Buck was on the bench, looking at his hands, as if he might find the answers in his palms. The social worker leaned in.

What did you say?

He whispered.

What?

She scribbled something, repeated it out loud:

Precariously housed.

◈

I took the long trip back through the night. At home, I hung my keys on the hook. Everything was still. I listened for a rustling behind the stove. Not even the roach was home.

I sat at the credenza. By the holiday lights. The notes. *Poetry Reading @ 6. Presentation: Tomorrow! Groceries: rutabaga (?) yogurt onions knives.* The screen saver glowed. I loaded a CD into my Discman and turned the volume up as loud as it would go. Disquiet sifted through the headphones, the opening bars to Brahms. They were a comfort to me now. I opened my email. There was the self-help author's name, in bold. A belated response to my anonymous request:

Dear Reader,

Thank you for your note. Can I ask, when you say you almost killed your husband, do you mean literally, or metaphorically? This seems to me the only distinction that matters. Anyway, I hope this helps.

S.

I searched for metaphors. None applied. I read the message again. I wished she'd taken *my* advice: Address us desperate people clearly, declaratively, avoid ambiguity at all costs.

I put my head in my hands and waited for sleep. I thought of going across the hall to Claire's, or downstairs to the self-help author's, to ask her in person what she meant. But there was nothing either of them could do. I reached for the phone. The line expired at the tone of the answering machine. *Hello, you've reached Insta-Ad.* I recorded a stretch of silence. A few nervy notes of Brahms. The machine had perfect female pitch. *If you are satisfied with your message* . . . I dialed two to delete.

Misha's bucket and wand stood by the door. I brought them into the kitchenette, for company. The equipment made a solemn still life in the corner. I regretted never having gone with Misha to search the Rockaways. I suppose I always was a landlocked woman, terrified at heart. At this juncture, however, I would have liked nothing more than to walk with him along the beach as the waves came crashing in, brimmed with violent froth. I imagined the mist, the chill, the vast navy of the ocean, twin wands hovering over the shore. The world was trash. There was never enough. Lower Manhattan was built upon it, we shipped whole landfills out to sea, on barges bellowing mighty horns. And yet how much remained for us to sift, to sort. The ghosts of shampoo bottles alighted on the shore. One could drown in all this trash. Misha and I walked for miles along the sands of my mind and in the end found nothing at all. Still I couldn't bring myself to stop. We were already so far along.

I navigated back to the search bar and typed in my own name. It was days since I'd checked in on my doppelgängers. There was the librarian. The porn star. The links had aged to deep claret, but there was also a new result, bright blue, that I'd never tried. I clicked. There was my name below the headline, *The Real Woman Behind* The Exhibition of Persephone Q. A picture of Persephone herself. I took a long look. Then I left her alone. She slept for all of us, it seemed. Meanwhile, the porn star was out there, sowing pleasure. The librarian, forgiving fees. The tilt of the earth, I thought, was sensitive to the indulgence in six pomegranate seeds. I reached for my keys and stood for a long while at the air shaft, looking up. It had no messages for me. Then I locked the door, stepped into the night.

Misha was outside, sitting on the steps.

You work of art, he said.

A NOTE ABOUT THE AUTHOR

Jessi Jezewska Stevens was born in 1990 in Lake Placid, New York, and grew up in Indianapolis. She holds a BA in mathematics from Middlebury College and an MFA in fiction from Columbia University. Her stories and essays have appeared in *The Paris Review*, *Tin House*, the *Los Angeles Review of Books*, *4Columns*, the *Harper's Magazine* blog, *Guernica*, *BOMB*, *The Rumpus*, and elsewhere. She lives in Brooklyn.